Mi Vida Loca
Trust
I0743787

THE NAUGHTY LIST

C.R. JANE

MILA YOUNG

CONTENTS

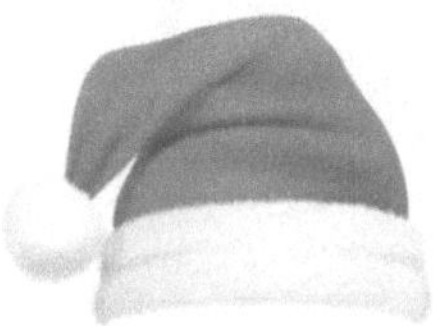

THE NAUGHTY LIST

We're going to spend the holidays getting me on Santa's Naughty List!

I've always been on the 'Nice' list. Never been one to stray too far from the beaten path, and I managed to make it to senior year without doing well... much of anything. Until I ended up stranded in Chicago during the worst snowstorm of the century, away from my family, and days before Christmas.
And then I meet them.
Two of the most insanely gorgeous guys I'd ever laid eyes on.
Charismatic. Sexy. Daring.
I've wanted to escape my life for Christmas for so long...and they offer me a chance I just can't pass up.
What else is a girl going to do while stranded in a strange city on her own?
They insist that they can get me into Santa's Naughty list in less than three days.
So, I accept the challenge.
But that's if I can keep my heart... I mean head, in the game.
Because losing my heart was never part of the rules...

NAUGHTY LIST #1: GET DRUNK IN THE MIDDLE OF THE DAY

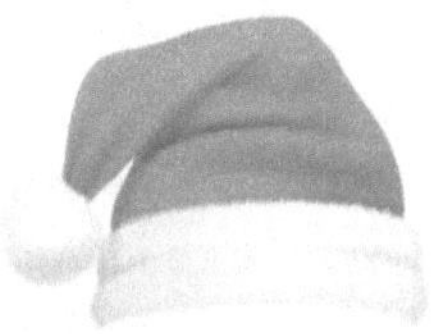

"Flight 793 to Chicago, will be boarding soon. Please make sure that you have all of your belongings with you," a robotic airline employee's voice said over the intercom.

It was Christmas break, something I'd been dreading the whole semester since it meant that I'd be returning home. A home that was the epitome of hell ever since my father had decided to remarry a woman who I was pretty sure doubled as Maleficent in her spare time. Add in her psychotic son and we were set to have a holly, jolly Christmas.

I picked up my shoulder bag and made sure that my carry-on was still in one piece. I had the luggage forever, and one of the zippers was broken. I was forever worried that all of my underwear was going to spill out in the middle of the airport one day...yet I never bothered to get a new one from a lack of funds.

I began to walk over to the gate entrance. I was one of those people that even though my zone would be one of the last called, I had to be ready. Flight anxiety, I guess.

As I weaved through the rows of chairs, I couldn't help but notice some eye-candy sitting over by the windows.

Eye-candy didn't really do them justice though. I was reasonably sure they were the most attractive guys I had ever seen. They were about as far apart in looks as possible. One was a blonde Adonis while the other one looked like a fallen angel with hair so dark that it almost looked blue under the airport's bad lighting.

They looked like they had been carved from marble with their bodies that were so good even under their clothes that I wasn't sure if they were real...I was drooling. I hadn't thought it was possible to actually see a six-pack through clothes, but the proof was right in front of me.

The dark-haired dreamboat caught me staring just then and shot me a wink with piercing blue eyes that threatened to do me in. I quickly averted my eyes and walked faster to where people were starting to gather to get in line. I could feel a hot blush creeping up my neck at the fact that he had seen me staring at him. Ugh.

First class was called and of course the two perfect specimens got up and strolled to the line. We wouldn't want them to have those looks and be poor.

I couldn't help but watch them as they headed down the tarmac. I felt a little bit like a stalker. They slipped out of sight, and I suddenly got antsy to get on the plane myself, just so I could stride by them again.

Get your crap together, I muttered to myself, causing an old lady in front of me to give me a sharp glance.

The airplane was almost full when they finally called my section, perks of buying the cheapest flight available...which honestly still wasn't that cheap since it was the holidays.

Someone bumped me from behind and I dropped my bag. The top of it ripped open, and I moaned when some books tumbled out. I was so flustered by the time I got on the plane, that I'd all but forgotten the two hotties from before.

That changed quickly when I began to walk through first class and saw them. The dark-haired one was already nursing a beer, and the blonde one held a tumbler in his hand full of some kind of amber colored drink, probably a fancy liquor.

It must be nice to have that kind of money, I thought to myself a little bitterly as my bag popped another stitch, threatening to spill its contents all over the aisle.

I tried to keep my eyes from gazing at them as I passed by, but of course I couldn't do that. They were both looking at me when I turned to gaze at them, and I was sure that my face turned a bright cherry red when our eyes met.

The dark-haired one winked at me again while the blonde just watched me stoically. I hurried past them, bumping the person in front of me who shot a glare over his shoulder. I was still blushing when I got to my seat. Of course, it was the middle seat in the very back row.

At least I won't have to go far for the bathrooms, I tried to reassure myself as I heard a toilet flush through the thin wall behind me.

I picked up my phone to check Facebook before the flight took off.

I had a message waiting for me from Todd, the creepiest

stepbrother you could imagine. He was a year older than me, but there was some kind of screw loose in his head. Whenever I went home for breaks, he always managed to be there as well. I couldn't tell you the number of times my butt had been groped passing him in the hallway and I always made sure to lock my door while I slept just in case he decided to creep in while I was sleeping. I shivered and deleted his message without reading it. *No, thank you.*

My thoughts flickered to the guys currently sitting in first class. Why couldn't my stepbrother have looked like one of them? Not that I would ever have done anything with a hot stepbrother to begin with, but...

I was the quintessential good girl. I'd really never done a darn thing out of line in my life. See, I couldn't even say the word d-a-m-n. Probably the naughtiest thing I'd ever done was to pick a college in California when my dad had wanted me to stay close to home.

Not that he cared about that after step-monster came into the picture.

I leaned back into my seat and sighed.

I had one semester of college left after I got back from Christmas break, and what did I have to show for three and a half years of angelic behavior? Nothing. My grades weren't even all A's.

My phone buzzed again just as the flight attendant reminded us to turn off our phones in preparation for take-off.

Can't wait to get close to you this break.

I gagged. It was Todd again. I didn't know what his deal was. Not responding once again, I turned off my phone and closed my eyes, trying not to lean too far left or too far right and bother my seatmates. The one to the left of me had a bad case of body odor. I opened my eyes once the smell got to be too much, and I leaned over to grab my bag, pulling out my favorite peppermint lotion. I knew it was bad etiquette to open something that smelled strong on an airplane, but I was fairly positive that everyone in these back rows would much rather smell "Holiday Peppermint" then my neighbor's smelly underarms.

The plane began to accelerate down the runway as I finished applying my lotion. Leaning back in my chair, I put on my headphones, turned on Taylor Swift, and settled in for the flight.

I woke up suddenly when it felt like the plane was falling out of the sky. My stomach rose up to my throat, and I looked outside. We were flying through a white-out. Far different than the sunny skies we had left behind in California.

I had never liked flying, especially in turbulence like this. I let out a small squeak when the plane shuddered once again. The seatbelt sign flicked on and an announcement came on just then from the pilot.

"Sorry folks, looks like we will be experiencing some turbulence until we get to Chicago O'Hare. The storms a lot worse than anticipated. Please stay in your seats and we'll let you know when it's safe to get up."

I began to grip my armrests for dear life as he finished. I loved how he had said "some" turbulence as the airplane once again felt like it was falling out of the sky. Another thirty minutes passed like this, and by the time the pilot announced that we were descending, my nerves were shot.

We landed, and I was so glad to be on the ground that I didn't even mind when my smelly neighbor let out a fart that sounded, and smelled, like it had come from an elephant.

When I stepped off the plane, I wanted to kiss the

ground. Looking out the windows of the airport I could see that this was a really bad storm. My flight to New York was probably going to be just as bad with turbulence. I shivered just thinking about it.

I grabbed a Starbucks, my favorite white chocolate peppermint mocha of course, and set off for my gate. Chicago O'Hare was huge, and it took me ten minutes to get there. As I walked up to the gate, I was dismayed to see that the flight had been delayed by two hours.

I walked over to the front desk to talk to the airline employee and get more details. There was a line of anxious people, all complaining about the delay to the stressed-out employee.

I moved closer to hear what she was telling everyone.

"Sorry, ma'am. Until we are given the all clear, all aircrafts are grounded. We are hoping the storm passes soon and flights can recommence. It's going to be at least a few more hours though," the flustered employee told the woman standing in front of her who looked like she was about to cry.

The employee's eyes flickered over to me and she smiled softly, probably a practiced smile she offered all commuters stuck here.

I decided not to bother her since she wasn't going to say anything different to me. I stepped aside from the crowd of people that continued to line up to hear the same terrible news. Looking through the floor to ceiling windows that all airports seemed to have, I watched the snow blanket everything in sight. The planes. The runway. The buildings in the distance. The wind howled, blurring the view with white dust. I shivered just looking at the horrible weather.

The storm of the century had hit the day I landed in Chicago, leaving me and everyone else stuck due to our delayed flight. So what now? From the looks of it and the weather report I had pulled up on my phone, it didn't seem like it was going to be a delay of just a few hours.

Glancing down at my phone, I sent my best friend, Myles, a quick message.

Stuck in Chicago. Flight to NYC delayed due to storm. Hope it's just a few hours.

...

I waited for her response to pop up.

The weather is nasty here too, but I'm sure it will pass soon. In the meantime, find a hot guy. Tell him you're not wearing any underwear then walk away. He'll buy you drinks all night to pass the time.

My cheeks flushed just reading the words, and I looked around in case anyone had read her reply over my shoulder. Myles always sent the most insane messages. I quickly typed back a response.

Don't tell me you've actually done that?

Maybe. But girl, you'll never guess who I saw at the mall today. Your douche ex, Liam.

I furiously typed back, my blood boiling just reading his name. The dick had cheated on me, then tried to blame me, and dumped me via text.

Let me guess, I typed. *He got into another fight?*

He was with this girl, but don't worry, she wasn't that pretty and had greasy hair. They were kissing, so I bumped into them and told her he's a pig.

I laughed to myself as I typed, *You go girl.*

"Oh, look she's smiling," a guy said, flirtatiously, and I glanced up to see the infuriatingly cute dark-haired guy from the plane with those blue eyes I could easily lose myself in.

"I'm standing right here. I can hear you," I answered, feeling like I was back in high school.

His friend with the blonde hair and sharp cheekbones that looked like they belonged on a movie star, nodded. "Pretty sure she's smiling because she's going to join us for a drink at the bar."

I rolled my eyes and snorted before turning back to my phone, although my cheeks were blushing from their attention. Myles hadn't responded yet but her suggestion on passing the time slid over my thoughts. I stiffened. Not in this lifetime. That wasn't who I was.

"What have you got to lose?" Blondie asked.

"Hmm let me see. My life if you two end up being serial killers."

Sexy Blue Eyes burst out laughing so hard that he teared up, drawing attention from the line-up of angry passengers. I mean, I couldn't deny that the sound of his laugh was the most delicious thing I'd ever heard. Loud, deep, and sexy as hell. Both of them were so hot it ought to be illegal.

"Thanks for that, Perky. I needed a good laugh." Blue Eyes' gaze dropped to my chest in a fleeting moment, and I resisted the urge to cross my arms.

"Excuse me?"

"Well, you haven't given us your name, and you seem to have a super "perky" personality," the Blonde replied, his green eyes staring at me with a secret hunger. His friend smirked; hands deep in the pockets of his jeans as he tried to recover from laughing so hard.

I narrowed my eyes at them, and I pushed aside the tingling in my gut that these two hot guys were actually talking to me. "You know you could ask me what my name is. How would you feel if I called you muscles and your friend...? I don't know." I glanced around for a clue as my mind was foggy in their presence and having two against one had me flustered. My gaze swept over a poster of a salad. "Cucumber," I blurted and the moment the word left my mouth, I froze. What had I been thinking? *Stupid. Stupid. Stupid.*

"I'd say you were very accurate," Blondie answered in a droll voice, his amused gaze never leaving me. I could feel the heat shooting up my spine and over my neck and cheeks. I wasn't sure if the fire was my embarrassment at these two for teasing me or just me daydreaming because two gorgeous specimens were talking to me. I would go with the first one even though it was a lie. Good thing I could give back as good as I got.

"I'm not in the mood for douchebags today, thanks." I spun on my heel with my beat-up handbag under my arm and dragged the wheelie onboard luggage behind me.

My body burned up from the inside out, and I felt their eyes on my back. Somehow, I ended up putting an extra swing in my hips before merging into the chaos of crowds...which was so unlike me.

Then I ran to the bathroom.

Who in the world did they think they were? Perky, please.

I stood in front of the full-length mirror near the sinks. My nipples were at full mast, pressed against my white shirt, and I almost died. Shit! I rubbed them with my palm until they settled down. My cheeks burned the color of a cherry, my hair was sticking upward on one side, and I had a black smear on one knee of my jeans. Kill me now.

Taking a huge breath of air, I quickly collected a paper towel, dabbed it with water, and cleaned the dirt off as best I could. Digging in my handbag, I pulled out my comb, taming my golden hair that always bounced with a loose curl over my shoulders. With the lipstick, I colored my lips a shade of nude with a hint of pink. Just enough to stand out, but not too much to look slutty.

I grimaced that I'd just recited Gloria's words. Gloria was the step monster and her insults and orders were always in my head even when I hadn't seen her for months.

I applied a few more layers of lipstick for a darker finish as a subtle "f.u." to the thought of her. There, now I looked fantastic.

Staring at myself in the mirror at my blue eyes, I couldn't help but think of my Mom. I hadn't taken after much of her looks with my curvy frame and average five-foot five height. She had been tall and thin, like a model.

But I had gotten her eyes. My dad had always told me after she passed that he saw her in my eyes every time he looked at me.

I leaned in closer to the mirror, swearing if I looked deep enough into my eyes, it felt like she was with me again. My breath misted the mirror. My heart clenched with sorrow because I missed her terribly, especially at Christmas. When she'd make her famous Portuguese turkey roast, decorate the whole house with way too many Santa Claus's, and insist we sang carols. I used to hate doing them, now... now I'd give anything in the world to hear her persistent voice, her excited voice, her loving voice.

I swallowed the lump in my throat when someone moved behind me. I quickly stepped back from the mirror, wiped away the loose tear, and tossed everything in my handbag. In haste, I made my way to the toilet.

Back in the main area of the airport, I strolled with my wheelie bag behind me, past crowds of people, looking into the big branded stores I could never afford. Each cafe I walked past was jam packed with a line out the door. When

I found no line in front of the sports bar, I marched inside to the bar, noticing people were everywhere. Large screens dotted the walls, playing all the latest sports, and the air smelled of beer and fried food. Perfect.

"What will you have?" a woman's voice asked, and I turned to find the bartender offering me a curt smile, clear she'd been run off her feet from the influx of stranded passengers.

"Too early in the day for a Margarita?"

She half chuckled. "Ma'am, in my books, it's never too early."

I rarely drank, but right now I felt like drowning myself in something delicious.

"Sounds perfect. Can I get the nachos too, please?"

"Absolutely. Take a seat, and I'll bring everything out to you."

"Thanks." I turned to find a table, even sharing with someone would be perfect, as long as I just got to sit in peace and work out my next steps. Except, every single chair was filled, even along the window with the single seats.

Someone waved to me from across the room at a tall table with three seats around it. Two of the seats were taken. The moment my eyes laid on those two arrogant jerks, my stomach dropped.

A smile crossed Blue Eyes' lips, and I shook my head, then walked towards the far window, figuring I was bound to find something. All I needed was one chair and I'd squeeze in another table. But it wasn't long before I realized that luck wasn't on my side, and I glimpsed over my shoulder at them. Both were staring at me, probably laughing, and I sighed.

"Hi, ma'am, where will you be sitting?"

I looked over to the lady from behind the bar holding

my margarita in a hurricane glass and a large plate of nachos.

Panic crawled through me as I looked around the room.

"Over here," Blue Eyes called from his table. "She's sitting with us."

"Okay then." The waitress marched toward them.

I eyed them with my best glare, but Blondie just winked.

They were going to make me suffer. I knew it.

Deep breath.

NAUGHTY LIST #2: TAKE CANDY FROM A STRANGER

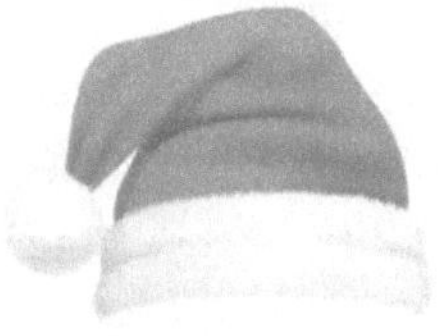

"Thank you," I said sheepishly, feeling their stares on me. I squirmed from the heat clinging to me once again. I climbed up on the stool, the plate of nachos in front of me, but I reached for the Margarita first, my hands shaky as I did so. I was never good with confrontation, or with guys in general. I was a mumbling mess in fact. And I'd never in all my life had two men as divine as these two take interest in me. Ever. So, having them look at me like I was their dessert had butterflies in my stomach beating their wings a bit too hard at the moment.

I took a big mouthful of the margarita, its delicious iciness sliding down my throat. I needed the alcohol to kick in fast. Maybe the trick was to pretend my previous encounter with them didn't exist. Pretend they were just friends and not the hottest guys I'd seen in my entire life.

"So, how'd you manage to score a table? This bar is crazy busy. Look at this place." Oh gosh, I was rambling. I drank some more. Who was I kidding... I couldn't pretend I was sitting with ordinary people and that I didn't want them. These two were the farthest thing from ordinary with their perfect faces, perfect kissable lips, perfect muscular bodies. And all I could picture was them against me.

Was my face burning up again?

I settled back in my seat to glance out the window, unsure where to look, trying to be cool. *Please, just clear up long enough for me to get home.*

The seat under me started to tilt backward.

Fear speared through my chest as my arms flayed outward to grasp the table, my eyes wide.

Blondie's hand lashed out and snatched my arm, pulling back up. "I got you."

"Oh, crap." I burst into a nervous laugh. Oh my god, kill me now.

"It was the only table left," he finally answered with a smile. "But if you don't like it that much, we can find another?" He swept a lock of his slightly too long hair off his brow. His voice was like candy... sweet, and I knew if I listened to him too long, I'd grow a new addiction. "I'm Max by the way. And this is my friend, Danny."

They both regarded me with welcoming smiles while I collected the Margarita for another gulp to help settle the inferno inside me.

"I'm Isabelle. But my friends call me Belle," I murmured. "You know like Belle in Beauty and the Beast."

"So, your parents named you after a Disney cartoon?" Max asked, mirth behind his words as he smirked.

"No, no," I replied quickly. "I don't even know why I said that, it just slipped out." What was wrong with me? I needed to shut up. Yes, that was a good plan.

"You'd be happy to know I was named after a famous dog," Max added seriously before swinging back a gulp of his beer from the bottle.

"A dog!" I blurted, staring at him incredulously.

Danny started laughing, the sound raising the hairs on my arms in all the best way. He nudged his friend. "Don't exaggerate. His name is really Maxwell." He looked at me with a bright smile, his white teeth beaming, his smile hinting at an easygoing nature, I could easily just listen...and look at them all day. "His younger sister used to call him Max after a TV show with a talking dog called Max, so the nickname just stuck."

"Yep, my name came from a famous dog."

I laughed, while they helped themselves to their bucket of wings. Maybe sharing a table with them wouldn't be so bad, and I helped myself to my nachos.

"Were you both in L.A. for holidays? Visiting friends? A girlfriend?" I asked, drowning in the rest of the Margarita, hiding behind the glass. Why couldn't I stop saying crap? And this was why I didn't go on dates because I jammed my foot in my mouth constantly.

"No. Yes. And no," Danny responded. "By the way, you're super cute when you're nervous. Guess it takes one to snow one."

I lowered the glass to meet his divine blue eyes, unsure if I just heard wrong. "Snow one?"

Max chuckled and slapped his friend on the back.

"Danny loves Christmas puns. I'm surprised he held off this long to drown you in them."

"Tis the season to be wild."

I half snorted a laugh. They were kind of funny.

Max started to climb to his feet. "What can I get you to drink?" he asked me. "Actually, leave it to me." He walked toward the bar.

I watched him walk away, at the muscles moving under his shirt, at the way his shoulders tapered to a narrow waist, and that ass. Hmmm... I chewed on my lower lip.

"What were you doing in L.A.?" Danny asked, drawing my attention to him wiping his fingers on the paper tissues.

"I'm a senior at USC. I'm majoring in commerce," I added, not knowing why I had added that.

He nodded and leaned forward. "Good university. And why commerce?"

"My parents brought me up saying I ought to have a good career before I settled down."

"I'm getting the whole good girl vibe with you. At first, I couldn't tell if it was an act, but now I'm thinking it's the real deal."

"And is that a problem?"

He chuckled and pulled back in his seat; hands raised in defense. "No problem at all. If anything, I'm intrigued how good you really are. Like if I used a pick up line, would your cheeks blush that gorgeous color, or would you put me in my place?"

"Depends on the pick-up line?" I responded...even as I blushed.

"Hmm." He stroked his chin, his gaze drifting to the ceiling. "I lost my number, can I have yours?"

"Is that your best?" I asked with a smile at how bad it was.

"I see your point," he said sarcastically, teasing me. "How about, kiss me if I'm wrong, but the dodo bird still exists, right?"

A laugh burst from my lips at that one.

"I'm getting warmer, aren't I?" Scooting closer to me in his seat, he leaned towards me. "And what if I said, did you know our tongue is the strongest muscle in our bodies?"

Warmth spread over my body at the way he whispered and implied so many unspoken words. "Then I'd be intrigued and probably Google it to make sure it was true."

That delicious grin returned, and he pulled back into his seat as Max returned. I felt trapped, hypnotized by his flirting. I blinked away the buzz inside me and let out a rushed breath. Was it getting hot in here?

"Drinks coming up soon," Max announced and took a seat, studying me with a raised brow. "Feel like I missed something fun." He offered me a lop-sided grin and it looked rather charming on him.

I shook my head; not sure I could repeat what Danny was saying... well maybe the dodo one as that was hilarious. "So, should I be scared about what you ordered?" I asked. "I'm not a huge drinker."

"You only drink what you like and how much you like, deal?" Max had this intoxicating way of speaking with that deep voice that drew me in, that made me want to sit and listen to him for hours.

"So our girl, Belle is a self-proclaimed good girl," Danny confessed.

"Technically that's not what I said," I corrected him.

"Yeah, I can see what you mean," Max's response came fast toward his friend.

"Hey, for all you know I rob banks in my spare time."

They exchanged bemused looks and shook their heads.

"Fine, I don't rob banks. But there's nothing wrong with wanting to be on Santa's good list."

Just then the bartender arrived with a silver tray and a collection of shots.

"That's a lot of drinks," I murmured.

"Got to pass the time somehow while we wait for our flight." Danny helped the woman fill our table with drinks as she collected their empty bucket of wings.

"You still going?" the lady asked, looking at my half uneaten plate of nachos.

I nodded. "I'm going to need it if I drink all this." There were twelve shots on the table. Four each. I'd pass out after one.

"*Icy* why you did that," Danny piped up. "You're ready to drink big."

The waitress giggled, glancing over at him with battering eyelashes. She was flirting with him hard, bending over slightly so he could see down her shirt.

When Danny didn't seem to notice, she headed back to the bar with a disappointed look on her face.

Max passed us each one shot glass. "This one is called the Christmas Cookie Shot. It's creamy and sweet, so a good one to start with."

I lifted it to my nose and my eyes lit up. "It does smell like a cookie."

Danny lifted his glass. "Here's to trying to get Belle on Santa's naughty list this year. We'll gladly take the position of your elves," he said in a sultry voice.

A thrill shivered down my spine and lower at the way he said that like they were under my command.

That little angel on my shoulder reminded me I was here with strangers, getting potentially drunk, and I should politely leave.

"That sounds perfect. Are you up for the challenge, beautiful?" Max asked. Both guys looked at me expectedly. Yeah, nothing like peer pressure. Except... what was I going to lose by having a bit of fun for once in my life?

The devil on my other shoulder insisted I'd been working hard all year...for years in fact, and that I deserved this.

A sharp beep came from my pocket, and I flinched, fumbling to pull the phone out of the pocket of my jeans.

It was my stepmother, Gloria, and I groaned. "Give me a sec, I have to take this."

Quick on my feet, I answered as I walked toward the entrance where it was quieter. "Hi, Gloria. Is something wrong?" She rarely called me.

"Belle, just wanted to make sure you don't miss your flight. Saw on the news a terrible storm has hit Chicago. And I know you have trouble staying on time, so I wanted to check on you."

I gritted my teeth at her passive aggressiveness. "All flights have been grounded. Don't worry, I'll make it home by Christmas." I now wished I'd turned down the invite.

"Good, good. I've ordered expensive catering and invited a few friends. So please don't let down your father."

Rolling my eyes, I bit my tongue instead of lashing out at her. "Okay, well I better go," I said. "Speak to you soon." I hung up and grasped the phone tight until my knuckles turned white.

I hated the way she spoke to me, how she always expected me to fail, and who did she think she was anyway? I turned to the sports bar and eyed my two tablemates who were chatting with a group of three women, who were flicking their hair and giggling. Where did they come from?

It shouldn't have bothered me, but a fire had ignited in

my chest at seeing them throw themselves at the guys, one of them reaching over and touching Danny's arm.

I headed back to the table, Max noticing me first and offering me a smile.

The girls didn't even move out of my way, so I shuffled around them to climb back into my seat.

A red-haired beauty eyed me and almost glared that I dared return. What was her problem?

She handed over a piece of paper to Danny and winked. "Call me," was all she said before her and her friends sauntered away.

"You're Mr. Popular," I said.

"'Tis the season to be jelly," he teased, but when he saw I wasn't laughing, he just reached over and ran a finger down my hand. It left a shiver of excitement in its wake, and then he scrunched up the note from the red-head and tossed it onto my plate that had somehow emptied while I was on the phone.

Max watched intently, and a strangeness crept between us. I had the urge to ask him what he was thinking. But that wasn't what this was. So instead, I said, "So, are we doing this or are you guys all talk? Let's have some fun and do our best to get me on Santa's naughty list."

"Ha, the challenge is on," Max said, raising the shot glass to his lips. Danny followed suit and we all swung back the creamy yumminess that awakened my senses. The strong hit of alcohol afterward had me giving my head a quick shake.

"That wasn't too bad." The heat traveling down my esophagus warmed me up deliciously. Another Christmas Cookie shot later, and I felt fuzzy in my head already.

Next, Max placed a red drink with a candy cane sticking out of it. "These are Candy Cane Jell-O shots," he explained.

"Oh, I haven't ever tried this either." And I was seriously excited to try it. Collecting it in my hand, I used the candy cane to dislodge some of the jelly and poured it into my mouth. The strength of Vodka hit first, combined with a raspberry flavor. "Oh, this is really delicious." I scraped the sides of the shot glass with my candy cane then stuck it into my mouth, sucking its goodness.

"Oh, that looks really good," Max teased. "I could watch you all day."

I popped the candy cane I'd been sucking out of my mouth and lifted my gaze to two sets of eyes watching me intently. In those few seconds, I knew that if I asked them to do anything, they'd show no hesitation. There was something empowering about having such sway over the attention of two guys like them.

"You want some?" I offered Max my candy, and he leaned closer, taking it into his mouth, his sexy lips closing in around it, grazing over my fingers.

A tremble of excitement shot up my arm and dove to the pit of my stomach and lower so fast, liquid heat roared to life inside me. I squeezed my thighs tight, and I fought the moan pressing on the back of my throat.

When his lips released the candy cane and he sat back, licking his lips, I could only stare, my mouth dry. "Now that is a great pick up line," I murmured to Danny who responded with a cocked eyebrow.

"So the dodo bird didn't do it for you?"

"Not even going to ask," Max said and reached for his jello shot.

"My head feels so fuzzy." I giggled and reached for the fourth drink, when Danny placed his hand on mine.

"How about we get some more of those nachos you were eating first to avoid getting sick."

He must have had the magic touch because the bartender had another order out to us within just a few minutes.

I pushed the plate in the middle of the table. "Will you share with me?"

He was already helping himself and I did the same. "I swear this is the best thing I've ever eaten! Oh my god, I think I'm drunk, and I regret nothing! I am all over this naughty list." I stuffed more food into my mouth, having the urge to laugh uncontrollably even as I faintly noted how ridiculous I sounded.

A crackling sound came from the speakers overhead and I looked up as if I'd see someone coming out of the speakers. That would be incredible if they did. I didn't remember the last time I felt so free and laid back.

"Passengers, we are sorry to inform you, but all flights have been cancelled for the rest of the day as the storm is predicted to intensify and spread towards the East Coast. We recommend making arrangements for the night. Please register on our app to receive a notification tomorrow on the status of flights."

"Crap!" I slouched in my seat, shooting a look out the windows where night had swept over the airport or was it just dark clouds?

Lots of passengers around us were grumbling, many already getting up and leaving.

I reached for my phone and did a quick search for hotel availabilities that didn't cost a fortune on my hotel app. My head was swimming from the drinks, and it was hard to focus.

No availability.

What the hell? I rechecked my search criteria, and hit enter again, convinced I made a mistake.

No availability.

"Crap."

"Hotels would all be booked out," Max told me. "Between the holidays and people temporarily booking rooms in case the storm got worse, I doubt you will find anything."

Why hadn't I thought of that?

"Well, looks like I'm sleeping here." I huffed and fiddled with the search criteria, widening the price bracket. I almost fell off my seat. The cheapest availability was for $800 a night. Were they insane? I wanted a gold bed for that.

"Belle," Max asked. "My dad's company has a suite permanently reserved in a hotel downtown for executives to stay during business trips. There's no one there right now so we can stay there. It's a suite with plenty of room, enough that you'll have your own bedroom. Why don't you come with us?"

"No, I couldn't impose," I quickly responded. Me sharing a room with strangers was out of the question, even if they were hot strangers.

Grogginess pulled at my limbs, and worry was now seeping into my bones. Without thinking I reached over and drank the last shot, needing to numb the dread consuming me.

"We're not leaving you here alone and drunk. You're coming with us," Danny said. "We give you our word we won't hurt you or go all serial killer on you, deal?"

I looked around at the now empty bar. I didn't want to be here alone. Didn't want to feel sorry for myself. So maybe it wouldn't be so bad to have some company during such a miserable storm. And sleeping in the airport wasn't fun. I knew that from when I had flown stand-by last year and had to spend the night in the airport when I couldn't get seats on any flights.

"Okay," I finally said. "But I'm messaging my friend the hotel details and your full names and cell numbers."

"Good." Max was on his feet, and I followed him, my knees wobbly. I was actually going with strangers to their room. I sent a quick message to Myles with what I was doing. Figured if she said run, get out of there, then I really shouldn't leave the airport.

My phone chimed in an instant with a response.

Yes! About freaking time. Did you use the no underwear line?

I rolled my eyes and tucked the phone into the back pocket of my jeans as I rushed up after my two new roommates.

We headed past the doors and toward Terminal 5. "Aren't we catching a cab?" noting that the signs said ground transportation was in Terminal 4.

"Trains are easier especially since our hotel is in Union Square and near the train station," Danny explained.

We sauntered slowly; my head still swam with alcohol. Maybe I shouldn't have had that last shot. My mind felt numb like I was having an out of body experience as we walked toward the free shuttle that would take us to the train station.

I was lagging behind, so Danny took my hand. "Come on, sweetheart. I don't want to lose you," he said in the sweetest voice.

I looked up at him, swooning. "You're so pretty, you know." Had I just said that out loud or was it in my head?

He chuckled; his grasp tight against my hand. "Never been called pretty before, but I'll take it."

I glued myself to them for the rest of the trip to the hotel. Even on the train, they had me sitting between the two of them, while I pointed at everything and couldn't stop laughing.

As we stepped off the train into the heart of Chicago, the whole street and buildings around us looked like a snow globe. The snow came down so thick, it reminded me of confetti. The streets were close to empty with only a few people rushing into stores or hotels. With Danny holding my hand tight, we ran out into the street. The winds lashed against me, and I squealed.

By the time we burst into the hotel foyer, I exhaled loudly. "The weather is insane."

"I'll be back." Max strolled to the reception desk while Danny and I stayed with the bags.

"This place looks classy," I murmured. It had a deep brown shiny floor, mirrors in gold frames lining the walls, all polished and almost glinting. There were flowers of every color in white vases in every corner, and there was a citrus vanilla smell in the air.

"How are you feeling?" Danny asked, drawing my attention to him. "Are you queasy or sick from the shots?"

I was shaking my head. "I feel like I'm flying," I told him in a sing-song voice. Something drew my attention to the right and I swung around to see someone walking the fluffiest Pomeranian across the foyer. I was bouncing on my toes and rushed over. "Hey, little guy."

The dog whipped around and exploded in a fury of barks. His fur bristled and he lunged at me, only held back by the leash.

I jerked backward, Danny at my back, an arm around my waist, catching me. "Whoa, that little guy is like Cujo."

The woman walking her pooch swooped him into her arms, glaring at me, before heading down a hallway.

"Did he get you?" Danny asked, turning me to face him

by my shoulders. There was a tenderness in his gaze I hadn't expected.

I spun to Danny. "Did you see the filthy look she gave me?"

Danny just nodded and gave a soft laugh.

Max returned, running a hand through his blonde hair. "Saw you upsetting that dog," he joked.

"Me," I feigned shock, pressing a hand to my chest and lurching on my feet before Danny caught me. "He was a vicious little thing."

"Sure he was," Max mocked me. "Let's go, our room is ready."

Up on the sixth floor, we walked down a narrow corridor with white walls and bowls of apples on every side table we passed.

"Just so you know, me coming with you guys to your room is definitely going on the naughty list."

"You bet," Max said with a grin as he inserted the key card and pushed open the door.

The first thing I noticed was the large windows and how big the living room was. An L-shaped black couch in front of a fireplace, a dining table with four chairs, and a small bar complete with a counter and the shelves stocked with booze. I didn't want to know how much it costs to stay here. Black and white paintings of the city of Chicago peppered the walls, making the place feel cozy.

"Wow, this is super fancy. How much are you paying for this again? We can split three ways." I toed my wet boots off, including the damp socks and tucked them near the shut door.

Danny dumped our bags near the sofa. "You're our guest. And like Max said, his dad's company pays for it. Go pick your bedroom."

I stilled. "Really?" I didn't even wait for him to respond, I rushed into the first one, which had two double beds with floor to ceiling windows, built in wardrobes, and the fluffiest white rug under my feet. I wriggled my toes and just breathed easy.

"I'm happy with this room," I called out, and grabbed my bag and wheeled it into the bathroom for a quick freshening up before anyone could say anything. I was apparently greedy when drunk.

The counter was filled with those cute bottles of shampoo and moisturizing cream. I loved them. Unlocking my bag, I pulled out my small toiletries bag. I did a quick toilet stop and refreshed my deodorant, followed by a quick spritz of my perfume. I pulled out my peppermint lotion that Myles had gotten me last Christmas and that had saved me on the smelly plane ride. This weather dried out my skin, so I lathered my hands and walked outside to see the guys already watching reruns of the World Series on TV.

Danny glanced over the couch at me, winking so sexily, that I burned up in an instant. It was like a tornado of fire, spiraling, coming right at me. And there was no way I could get out of its way. "You may want to check out the other bedrooms before you make a call," he suggested.

Curious, I wandered over to the next one and skidded to a halt in the doorway. "Holy monkey balls!"

Danny chuckled behind me.

An enormous king size poster bed consumed most of the room. Two walls of windows, and more lush rugs. I rushed inside and jumped on the bed, sliding over the covers. In the corner stood a thin tall white Christmas tree dripping with blue and silver baubles and tinsel. My insides fluttered at seeing this room. It was paradise and I wished my dorm back at the University was a quarter as good as this.

I snapped upright to a sitting position. "These are silk." My head was spinning right then and trying to think rationally was completely out of the question.

The more I saw of the hotel suite, the more I couldn't help but think this hotel would be very much out of my price range. Was this one of those thousands of dollars a night hotels? Who exactly were these guys to afford this?

I collapsed onto my back, waiting for my head to settle down. "Everything's spinning."

"How about you take a break and I'll bring your bags. Maybe just lay down until your head settles."

"Okay," I called out to Max, not moving as things seemed to settle down if I lay still.

"Yep, just leave me hanging with my ornaments." I burst out laughing. "See what I did there Danny. You'd appreciate that."

His sexy laugh faded into the other room, and I continued to lay there, unable to remember the last time I felt so relaxed, so happy.

It surprised me how much I enjoyed their company, and maybe just maybe, the layover may be better than I had ever dreamed.

My phone beeped with a message, and I pulled it out from my pocket, half expecting Myles again after I sent her the hotel and guy's details while on the train. But it wasn't her.

Dream of me, little sis. Love heart emoji.

I wanted to be sick, and the food and drinks I'd just eaten churned in my gut.

My stepbrother creeped me out and I loathed the way he looked at me like I was a piece of meat. I hated how he tried to touch my hand or shoulder or hair whenever he was near. It was completely and utterly wrong as I had told him on multiple occasions to stop it. He and Gloria made sure that I wouldn't ever look forward to going home for the holidays again.

NAUGHTY LIST #3: BECOME A VOYEUR

I turned over and burrowed myself into the warm, lavender scented sheets, so relaxed, I never wanted to get up. Memories came rushing over me just then, the airport, the two hotties, their hotel.

My eyes popped open and I gazed out over the horizon through the enormous windows to a drizzle of snow outside, all you could see in the distance were snow clouds. With the Christmas tree in the corner, I felt like I might have woken up in Santa's bed in the North Pole. Or I was still dreaming. Regardless, this hotel was spectacular.

Groaning, I pushed myself out of bed to find I still wore my clothes from yesterday. When I grabbed my phone from my pocket, it showed I'd slept all evening and night. Damn, after those shots I must have just dozed off.

I padded to the closed door and pulled it open to peer outside.

The living room was empty, and from the other rooms, I heard the soft snores from at least one of the guys.

I felt bad that I called them serial killers when they kept me company and offered me a place to stay so easily, although I guess they still could turn out to be dangerous.

Maybe I'd try to make it up to them by paying for a nice breakfast to be brought up.

Tiptoeing across the room, I headed to the bathroom, figuring first thing's first. Shower, grab my bag from the bathroom where I left it last, and then find out the status on flights.

A whiff of peppermint reached me... my peppermint lotion. I recognized that smell everywhere because it had a slight hint of vanilla and was unique.

The bathroom door was slightly ajar, the lights on, and I froze. Was someone even in there? I craned my neck to look inside without getting closer because I didn't want to catch them on the toilet or in the shower. Well, I lie, maybe a sneak of them in the shower might be a huge perk.

My cheeks warmed up at the thought. Yep, this would end up on the naughty list for sure.

I stepped closer and through the reflection of the mirror, I saw Danny standing there, completely naked and his back to the door. So many muscles had me blushing, frozen in place, staring at him. His head tilted back, eyes shut, a hand on his cock, pumping back and forth ferociously.

My mouth dropped open and my heart hit the back of my throat. I couldn't keep my gaze away as it traveled the length of his spectacular, strong body. From my angle, I could barely make out his cock as it was covered by his hand thrusting nonstop. Hell, I was officially deviant number one on Santa's naughty list now. But he was going at it.

Seeing Danny this way literally took my breath away.

I almost tripped over my own feet, my cheeks heating with a violent fire. Then I spotted my peppermint lotion bottle sitting open on the bathroom counter.

Was he really using it to...

I backed up slightly, unable to stop staring, wishing I had the bravado to walk in and help him. But I might faint if I tried from how fast my heart was racing. In slow motion, I went back to my room when the floorboard under my foot groaned. Panic soared through me. I lunged out of the room and shut the door as silently as possible. Without a thought, I ran to my bedroom and threw myself into the bed, hauling the blanket over me.

Dragging in jagged breaths, I laid there, overheating, my body tingling all over. All I could picture was Danny's euphoric face as he jacked off. That was officially the first time I'd seen a guy do that, and well... it was kinda hot. Hell, who was I kidding. It was panty-melting hot. Now all I could picture was him coming to check up on me in the room, wearing nothing. I wanted a full frontal.

What was wrong with me? I was blushing wildly now. How was I ever going to face Danny again without turning red? Without picturing him beating off.

My hands roamed over my breast, picturing Danny's hands on me. Fingers pinched my nipples tight, and a faint moan slipped past my lips.

"Tell me you're mine tonight," he'd ask.

"Yes, just for tonight." The words were barely a whisper, and I shivered with intensity.

"More than one night," he'd growl in my ear, his mouth

on my neck, hands sliding over my body. "Every night you'll be mine."

I traced my hand down the valley of my breasts and popped open my jeans. Fingers snuck in under the elastic of my underwear, over my small mount and against my clit.

A storm of arousal was shuddering through me as I rubbed myself. I inserted a finger inside me. But it wasn't enough... just not enough.

I pressed a thumb to my clit and rubbed as the desire rose and rose to where only my heartbeat sounded in my ears. All I pictured was Danny's head between my thighs, his mouth devouring me. Tension finally broke, my toes curled, and I swallowed the scream of my orgasm. I rode the pleasure that rocked through me in waves, holding on to make it last as long as possible.

Pulling my hand free, I lay spent on the bed, my pulse thumping with each heartbeat, and I chewed on my bottom lip, unable to believe I'd got so turned on by seeing him jerking off that I did the same. I'd be mortified if anyone ever saw me doing this.

I curled over in bed and waited for when enough time had passed that I was certain Danny would be finished, then I needed a shower to cool off.

By the time I heard them speaking, I got out of bed and walked out of my room, rubbing my eyes to feign that I'd just woken up.

"She's alive," Max announced with the cutest smile. His blonde hair was wet and slicked off his face, having that fresh face look that made him dreamy.

How could I be so attracted to two guys anyway? They were simply helping me out and wouldn't be interested in someone like me.

"Can't remember the last time I slept so long, but I feel great."

Danny eyed me, and all I could picture when I looked at him was his muscles, so much nakedness, and how boiling hot sexy he looked jerking off.

"How did you two sleep?" I held Max's stare as he shrugged.

"My pillow was lumpy."

"I'm feeling pine," Danny said, smirking.

"Your puns are growing on me," I admitted, my cheeks instantly heating up when I looked at him, so I lowered my head. "Well, I better have a quick shower, then I'm taking you out for breakfast."

In the bathroom, I noticed my peppermint lotion had been screwed back on and tucked near my toiletries bag where I'd left it last. I wasn't sure how to feel that he had used my lotion. A bit insulted or secretly happy he chose it for his pleasure?

Shaking my head and telling myself that I needed to get my head on straight, I jumped into the shower.

When I finished, dressed in jeans, several layers of tops and my long coat, my blonde hair blow dried; I was ready to eat something.

"I am so hungry," I admitted.

"Got some bad news." Max looked up at me, worry sliding over his expression.

"It's the storm isn't it?"

He nodded. "It was so strong last night and icy that all planes are grounded today and probably for another day or so."

I sighed. "Are you two planning on staying in town, or--"

"We've got a room, so we're bunkering down here and enjoying Chicago." Danny's blue eyes seemed to sparkle, and he seemed to always be in a good mood. I liked that about him. Heck so far I liked everything about both of them.

"So, I can stay with you both until the planes are back up? I'll pay for dinners, I doubt I could afford this place, but I can pay for other things?" I quickly blurted.

"Snow thank you," he murmured, eliciting a smile out of me. "Your company is plenty enough, and I do believe we've been tasked with putting you on Santa's naughty list, so we have a few days to achieve this. Unless you're the one backing out now." He raised a brow.

I scoffed at him. "As if. This is my chance to be someone else for a few days." I regretted my words as they flew past my lips, especially with the looks on their faces like I'd just dared them. "I mean, we don't have to go wild or anything."

Danny broke out into a dramatic malevolent laugh, and I rolled my eyes.

"Okay, let's go get some food."

Max joined me to leave the hotel room, while Danny kept cackling behind us.

There was something about these two that made me feel at ease, like I could trust them even though I barely knew them, and well there was also the obvious attraction. I couldn't get that aspect out of my mind. And after this morning's incident, I couldn't get the image out of my head no matter how hard I tried.

Chicago was freezing. It was the kind of cold that seeped through your clothes no matter how warm your coat was, or how many layers you had on. The hotel was situated right by the river. It was the perfect location as it was just a block from Michigan Avenue.

Despite how cold it was, after breakfast at one of the

hotel's restaurants, or more like early lunch since it was almost noon, we decided to walk to Michigan Avenue.

I blew into my gloved hands, as if that would somehow help to warm me up. It wasn't negative degrees yet, but it was a lot colder than New York ever got.

Danny threw an arm around my shoulder, and the feel of it changed the cause of my shivers from the weather to how good it felt for him to touch me.

Both of these guys had my stomach twisting up in knots.

"Belle," I heard my name from behind me. Danny and I stopped and turned around. I had thought that Max was right behind us, but he had stopped a little ways back. He was standing by a snowdrift that was separated from the sidewalk by a small alleyway. I guess the Chicago snow plows had decided that was the best place to push the snow.

"Get over here," he ordered in that intense voice of his. I was an independent woman, but some primal part inside of me responded to the authority in his voice and I was getting goosebumps just from the sound of it.

I could only imagine what he would be like in the bedroom. And those earlier shivers from the morning returned. I swallowed quickly and tried to push the thoughts aside.

Stop thinking like that, I ordered myself.

"Let's go see what Scrooge wants over there," Danny joked, taking my hand and pulling me after him towards Max.

"You called," I asked wryly, the sass in my voice making Max's eyes spark as if he was thinking of ways to punish me. Once again delicious shivers passed over me that had nothing to do with the cold. In fact, I was starting to feel quite toasty.

"I thought of the next thing you should do for your list,"

he said. I cocked my head, not seeing anything around that would make me particularly naughty. The sidewalk right outside the wall was crowded with people walking to lunch or back to work.

Danny crouched down and gathered up some snow that he began to pack into a ball. He stood up and handed it to me.

I scrunched up my nose. "What am I supposed to do with this?" I asked him, perplexed.

He gestured beyond the wall to the rows of business men and women walking nearby. "You are going to throw that snowball at them," he said matter-of-factly.

My stomach clenched. "No. That's not happening," I said, beginning to back away.

Danny stepped up behind me so I couldn't get away. "You told us you wanted to live a little," he reminded me gently in my ear. "You told us that you wanted to get on Santa's naughty list this year," he said. "Taking a few shots in the airport bar isn't gonna get you there."

My mouth gaped open like a fish. He was right, but I hadn't exactly been envisioning throwing snowballs at adults when I said that. I didn't actually know what I had been thinking of, but certainly not this.

"You gotta start somewhere," Max said, the challenging look on his face. "If you can't do this, I doubt you're gonna be able to do anything really naughty," he said with a smirk. "Come on princess. I dare you."

The taunting way that he said it riled something up in me, especially because of how naughty I had been earlier that morning. Not that they would ever find out about that. "Okay, I'll do it," I said, causing Danny to give a hoot of joy from behind me.

"Tell me I can do this without someone seeing?" I said

worriedly as I took the snowball in my hand. "The sidewalk looks too slippery for me to be able to run away," I noted, looking at the chunks of snow everywhere.

"That's just a risk you're gonna have to take." Max winked, seeming to love how much I was squirming.

Danny had his arms around my shoulder again. "They shouldn't be able to see you behind this wall, little bell," he told me reassuringly. "I used to always hide behind things during snowball fights growing up and they never caught me," he said proudly.

"Except the difference was you were probably eight when you were doing that," I noted.

"Are you going to do it or not? You can't delay forever," Danny prodded.

I huffed. "Okay, fine. Here goes nothing."

There was a man walking past us, looking close to our age. I figured that he would have a better sense of humor than the grizzly older businessmen around him. Reaching back my arm I threw it forward... And missed.

"Oh, shit," Danny muttered laughingly, pulling me behind the wall when my snowball missed my target but hit a particularly mean looking titan of industry type fellow. It smacked him right in the chest, splattering snow all over his face.

Even Max had a smile on his face at the sight. "You did it," he said, almost disbelievingly.

"Keep your voice down," I muttered to him, sure that the man was going to come after me seeking retribution at any moment. Danny peeked his head around the wall. "He's already gone," Danny said confidently.

I breathed a sigh of relief. "Why did you look so surprised?" I asked Max, remembering the look on his face.

"Didn't you ask me to do that, or did you have an expectation that I wouldn't?"

"I didn't think you would throw a snowball at a random stranger when taking a shot at an airport bar was an act of courage for you... I just didn't think you could do it."

I stuck out my tongue at him, realizing that somehow in the last ten minutes I had reverted back to my childhood...throwing snowballs and such.

He threw his head back and laughed, surprising me and Danny evidently. It was a beautiful, throaty laugh, made all the better because I knew that it didn't happen often.

We walked through the streets and wandered into stores for the next couple of hours until the sun started going down and Danny whined.

"I'm hungry."

Max rolled his eyes. "You're always hungry."

Danny patted his perfectly muscled stomach. "I want cookies... and milk," he said ridiculously.

I snorted. "Then I can sit with Santa?" I joked. Danny just smirked at me. He threw his arm around me once again and walked with me towards a restaurant I had never heard of. *Grand Lux Cafe.*

"This place is like Cheesecake Factory on crack," said Danny delightedly.

"I wanted to take you to Gibson's Steakhouse," said Max, frowning at the place Danny had picked.

"We can take her there tomorrow," Danny suggested. "They definitely don't have milk and cookies there."

We walked into the restaurant, and the guys garnered stares like they had everywhere we had been so far. But this time I was getting stares as well. Some of the women looked jealous. I realize how this looked, me tucked between two ridiculously hot guys. Anyone would think I was a lucky girl.

Dinner was amazing. I'd only been to Cheesecake Factory once a long time ago so I couldn't really compare the two, but the chicken dish I ordered and the cheesecake that followed were both really good. As we walked out Danny was practically jumping in place. "Where we going next?" he asked.

I looked at him in shock. "Um, to sleep?"

Danny just laughed at me and Max shook his head, that smirk he always had on his face. "You really don't know us well if you think we are going to sleep at eight pm," Danny said. He took his phone out of his pocket and started to fiddle with it. "Aha," he said delightedly. "A karaoke bar. We're going there next."

"But..." I started to protest, thinking of just how out of place I would be in a karaoke bar of all places. I had never been able to sing. The guys would not want anything to do with me if they saw me singing.

"Well that settles it, we're going," Max ordered. I stared at him incredulously. I somehow couldn't imagine him at a karaoke bar either.

He seemed so serious.

"You can't deny me a karaoke bar," begged Danny, reminding me of a dog who wanted a treat. I couldn't say no to him.

"Guess we're going," I answered with a reluctant shrug.

A cold breeze swished past, and it felt like it was -30°. I'd die out here.

We all headed toward the bar when my phone chimed with a message. I grabbed it from my pocket and glanced at what it said.

It was Todd. I cringed as I read his message.

Heard you were stuck in Chicago. Where are you staying?

I was not about to tell him. I knew he went to a state school somewhere in Illinois and I was not going to risk him somehow showing up if he hadn't been able to make it to NYC either. My break from reality included a break from dealing with him.

I stuffed the phone back into my pocket and joined the guys who waited for me outside of the Uber that had just showed up. Yep, I was going to have fun, and nothing would ruin that for me.

NAUGHTY LIST #4: EMBARRASS MYSELF IN PUBLIC

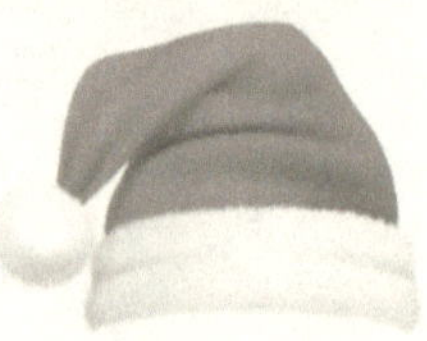

Goosebumps were erupting all over my skin as we sat in the Uber. I was in the middle, sandwiched between two guys who were more attractive than anyone I've ever seen. I had gotten somewhat used to Danny's penchant for being all up in my space, but Max seemed to be purposely sitting as close to me as possible as well.

I couldn't deny that I liked it.

We pulled up to a karaoke bar that apparently was very popular considering the line that wrapped down the street in front of it. I didn't know if that was usual for a karaoke bar since I had never been to one, I really hadn't been to many bars at all now that I thought about it.

When we got out, I started to head towards the end of

the line, but Max took my hand in his and marched us up to the front of the line.

"The end of the line is that way," the bouncer drawled in a bored voice as he put his stamp on a girl who was wearing very little considering the fact that it was many degrees below freezing right now.

Max reached into his wallet and cleared his throat, getting the bouncer's attention since we hadn't moved yet. He pulled out a few hundreds and slipped it to the bouncer who immediately let us in despite the protests of the people in line.

My mouth dropped in shock.

Had he really just dropped a few hundred dollars to get us into a karaoke bar? I couldn't fathom being that free with money. We had never been poor, just comfortable. Living in New York City where everything cost a million times more than everywhere else had always kept us on a strict budget. Especially now that my father had married a woman who didn't know the meaning of a budget, nevertheless a strict budget, the money that my dad sent for expenses in college was slimmer than ever. I had gotten jobs on campus to make ends meet, but I still couldn't imagine doing what Max had just done.

"Your mouth is going to get stuck like that," Danny chided as he tapped my chin gently to close my mouth, sending goosebumps down my neck.

I opened my mouth to say something, but Danny shook his head. "Just have fun," he told me quietly, making sure that his voice was out of listening range of Max who was going to the bar to get us drinks. "He just wants to show you a good time."

"You don't have to spend money on me for that," I said. "We just met."

"Max likes to take care of people, you just need to let him. He gets that from his dad, I guess," Danny explained. He paused for a moment as he seemed to search for what he wanted to say. "Think of it as his... love language if you will," he continued.

The word "love" made my stomach feel funny. I pushed the word quickly out of my head. I had no business even thinking about a word like that after knowing these guys for one day. I refused to admit to myself that they were the kind of guys who you could love though.

"Okay," I said softly. It had been a while since someone had wanted to take care of me. I was a senior in college who had only ever had one boyfriend in her life. It wasn't because guys didn't try. But when you had already been so disappointed by your dad, you were always on the watch for the same characteristics in the people you dated.

I had dated Liam my sophomore year, thinking that he was a safe option. He was studious, and he was pre-med. The fact that he was studying so hard I thought was a good thing. Because it meant that I would be able to keep up with my studies too.

Little did I know that he was actually "studying" the anatomy of his biology female classmates quite regularly. I only found out when I had stopped to drop him off a little study treat because he told me he had a big test. Finding him balls deep in a cute little brunette with a bubble butt had been a surprise. I knew she had a bubble butt because she had been riding him. Huge surprise to say the least.

When I wasn't actually that sad about his betrayal, I realized he had been a mistake to begin with. Since then I'd only gone on dates here and there, choosing to keep on the safe route.

"You still there?" asked Danny, popping me on the nose

to get my attention. I realized I had somehow managed to go off into Lala land in the middle of our conversation. I wasn't sure how I had done that in a crowded club.

I shook my head. "Sorry," I told him.

"You're doing that thing where you think too hard," observed Danny. "You're supposed to be on a break from reality, remember?" he said pulling me closer to him and causing my breath to hitch as I felt him harden against me. The feel of it reminded me of his little session this morning and how there had been nothing "little" about it. My face started to flush at my thoughts. He cocked his head at me, trying to study my reaction. He was just about to ask me something when Max appeared. "We have a table," he said looking between the two of us suspiciously. Surprisingly he didn't seem too upset about our proximity.

We walked to a table that was right in front of the stage. "Santa's elves coming in clutch," Danny joked, before Max punched him on the shoulder.

"Ouch, I thought that one was pretty good," he said. Max rolled his eyes but there was a little smirk on his lips. I wondered, not for the first time, how these two had become friends. Maybe they needed each other to balance each other out. Just from the little I had seen it seemed that it was almost impossible for Danny to take things seriously, while Max was the exact opposite. He took everything much too seriously.

"What are you singing tonight, Max?" Danny said leaning back in the leather bench that surrounded the table. I looked over at Max, surprised. "You're going to sing?" I asked. That was the last thing I'd expected from him.

Before Max could say anything, Danny jumped in. "Our Max here has mad skills. He also has a secret love for karaoke that he only gives into when we are away from campus," he explained.

Max left the table just then without adding anything to the conversation. I watched as he walked over to the DJ and started to look through the songs that were available to sing. He must've found one because he pointed, and the DJ nodded her head. She was an attractive brunette with streaks of bright blue in her hair. I tried to ignore the jealousy I felt when she leaned in closer to talk to him, revealing an enticingly large chest, right in his face.

"Someone feeling a bit jealous?" Danny whispered in my ear.

"I don't know what you're talking about," I said as I picked up a bottle of vodka that had just been delivered to our table by a pretty waitress. I quickly poured myself a shot and dropped it back, wincing as it burned my throat.

Danny handed me a glass of diet coke and I gulped it down.

"Easy killer," he said. I was already feeling lightheaded just from the one shot. Max came back just then. He rubbed his hands together, seeming more excited than I'd seen him look.

"What song did you choose?" I asked, curious about what music he liked.

"We'll just have to see," he said with a very uncharacteristic wink.

We watched a couple of singers. This was not like any karaoke that I'd seen. Everyone seemed to be really good. Where are all the drunk people who couldn't hold a tune?

It was finally Max's turn, and he walked up to the stage, confidence oozing out of every pore. I was struck again by just how good-looking he was. He was wearing a perfectly fitted black button up, with dark jeans. The top two buttons of his shirt were unbuttoned and for some reason that golden skin peeking out made me feel more feverish then I would if I saw someone else without any clothes on.

The music started and I laughed as Max started to perform, "Luck Be A Lady." His tone was perfect, but the song was so different from what other people had chosen that once again I'm left awestruck. Danny looked delighted, but not surprised.

"Did you know he was going to perform this?" I asked.

Danny smirked. "I knew it was going to be one of Frank Sinatra's songs. For some reason Max has an affinity for the rat pack."

Max had the girls in the crowd screaming...and some of the men. He added in a couple of smooth dance moves that could rival Justin Timberlake and I was feeling the heat.

Danny whispered in my ear just then, distracting me. "I have a dare for you," he said.

"And what would that be?" I asked, a mix of anticipation and dread filling me at the same time.

"You're going to go up there and perform a Christmas song," he stated matter-of-factly. I looked at him in horror. "You do not want to hear me sing," I tell him. "I'm not trying to get out of this because I'm scared, I truly sound like a dying animal when I try to."

He just smirked in that infuriatingly hot way of his. "That's your dare. Surely you're not going to back down now after you threw a snowball at an old man earlier today."

"He wasn't that old," I objected.

If you only knew what the bravest thing I actually did was in the last 24 hours, I think to myself as my insides tremble from the thought of what I had caught Danny doing that morning. What I'd done afterward had me blushing wildly.

Looking around the room, I reminded myself that I

didn't know anyone here. That was the whole point of this little adventure of mine. I could be who I normally wasn't because no one in my life was around. The crowd wasn't going to like my performance, that was for sure. But even if they booed me off the stage... who cared?

With that little pep talk under my belt, I turned to a triumphant looking Danny. "Okay, I'll do it," I announced to him.

His grin grew even wider, catching me off guard with the pure perfection of it. Our waitress had just come to the table and she stumbled a little bit from watching it. *I don't blame you*, I thought to myself.

Max came back to the table, a glint of sweat on his forehead that somehow only made him more attractive. "Well, what did you think?" he asked cockily, knowing he had been amazing. I gestured to the crowd that was still clapping and roaring after his performance. "I'm pretty sure you're getting enough adulation," I told him sarcastically.

Now they were both grinning at me. And I felt like I was about to hyperventilate. It was not fair that these two had been given this much charisma to go along with their hotness. I found myself waving a hand in front of my face to cool it down, and they both laughed even harder.

Grumbling, I slid out of the bench seat of the table and walked over to the DJ stand to pick a song. The DJ did not look as happy to see me as she had been to see Max. Again, I didn't blame her.

"What are you going to sing tonight?" she asked disinterestedly.

"What Christmas songs do you have?" I asked. She rolled her eyes and handed me a thin binder from behind her. I opened it up and scrolled through the songs. What song was least likely to cause eternal embarrassment... Hmmm. I found, 'Let It Snow' in the binder, and I giggled. Danny had already made plenty of snow jokes, might as well play into it.

"This one," I told her, pointing at the song. She smirked. "I'm guessing you're going to be the funny performance of the night," she told me.

"If by funny, you mean terrible," I responded with a laugh. She gave me her first genuine grin of the conversation. "I'm going to enjoy this," she said. She reached behind her again and came back with a Santa hat. "Here you go," she told me.

"Thanks," I said with a laugh as I placed it on my head.

"I'm bumping you up to next," she said with a smirk.

I nodded. "Might as well get it over with," I agreed.

The girl in front of me finished, someone who had pipes that resembled Mariah Carey of course. She came off the stage to roaring applause.

And then it was my turn.

I walked up the stairs to the stage shakily. The club wasn't that big, but it was packed. Seeing everyone in the crowd made me want to run away, but then my eyes flickered across Danny and Max's apt faces. Danny still had a challenging look on his face.

I took a deep breath. *I could do this*; I was going to fulfill this dare.

The music began and I started singing. I hadn't been exaggerating when I told Danny just how terrible of a singer I was. My voice was a combination of nails across a chalkboard and a wheel that was broken on a bicycle and needed oil. Danny and Max were literally falling out of their seats they were laughing so hard.

The audience was dumbstruck that someone so bad could actually be on stage singing, but their reactions just made me belt my heart out more. When the last notes faded there was silence as the crowd absorbed the train wreck they had just seen.

And then everyone started clapping, even as they laughed and wiped their eyes because come on...that took some nerve to be that bad publicly.

I got off stage as quick as I could, my cheeks flushing.

"That was amazing," crowed Danny once I got to the table. He was still rubbing his eyes from laughing so hard. "That was without a doubt the worst performance I've ever seen. I don't think anything can top it. Just brilliant, really," he said, still chuckling to himself at just the memory of it.

I looked over at Max to gauge his reaction, and his look wasn't what I expected. He was watching me like he was going to eat me. The blush that I was still rocking after my performance only got worse. The pompous prick smirked at me knowingly. He trailed his tongue over his bottom lip, wetting it, and I felt tingles everywhere.

"Why don't we get out of here?" he suggested in a silky voice.

Danny looked over at him. "That made you want to eat her milk and cookies. Didn't it?" he said with a grin. He looked at me and waggled his eyebrows. "Evidently bad karaoke makes Max want to 'rock around your Christmas tree,'" he continued.

Max and I both groaned. These were truly terrible puns.

"The least you could do is come up with good ones," I told him as we walked out of the bar. We stood on the freezing sidewalk waiting for our Uber. Luckily the bar had heaters set up outside so hypothermia didn't set in.

"Oh, like you could think of better ones?" challenged Danny.

I scoffed. "I'm pretty sure anyone could think of better ones," I told him.

Danny looked delighted at our banter. "Okay, let's hear them then," he said, crossing his arms in front of him.

"I'll give them to you in time," I responded, giggling. "It needs to be the right moment."

Danny's face lit up as he thought of something.

"What is it?" Max asked with a groan.

"I just thought of some good ones...but I'll be using them later," he said as he smiled somewhat lecherously.

Max and I both groaned again. "You both sleigh me," Danny muttered in response. The Uber chose to arrive at that moment, and we all got in, me with a huge smile on my face.

Back in the hotel room, Max went to the bathroom, while Danny fiddled with turning on the electric fireplace. I crashed on the couch, unable to believe the day I'd had. I hadn't felt this good, had so much fun in so long. And being with these two men came with those butterflies in my gut, like we were on a date and I couldn't wait to spend more time with them. Since when had I gone from serial killers to admiring them so much, I was comfortable to lounge around with them in their hotel room?

The flame flicked to life, sending an orange glow over the room. Outside the snow was coming down, the wind whistling while we were snuggled up in here.

Danny just stood there, warming his back, staring at me with a strange expression I couldn't work out.

"What is it?" I asked.

"Just thinking about something."

"And that is?" I cooed, loving how just talking to them had me humming with excitement.

"Have you ever heard of an eye for an eye?"

I squinted at him. "Yeah, but this is starting to sound kind of ominous now."

"Well, I was just thinking about this morning." He eyed me suspiciously.

My stomach dropped, followed by my mouth at the thought that he had seen me spying on him masturbating in the bathroom. "You knew!"

His mouth pulled into a wicked grin, and I burned from the inside out, my face blushing furiously as embarrassment shot through me.

I couldn't find my words, but what came out was not what I'd intended. "You've used most of my peppermint hand lotion."

He laughed, and it was wrong how divine he sounded, how much he sent my body into a tingle of excitement.

"It smelled like you, but don't change the topic. You got to see me, so only fair you now offered me the same pleasure."

"No! Are you insane?" I blurted, my heart hammering in my chest. I would die if I ever did that. The blood drained from my face. I couldn't breathe.

"Should I go get your lotion?" he asked, with a naughty grin, and I just wanted the world to open up and swallow me. "We can do it now."

"Do what now?" Max entered the room, strolling like he was the king, and okay, he looked like he could be.

But I was melting right now and wanted to hide.

"Why's your face so red?" he asked.

My breaths were coming so fast, and the room tilted beneath me. What Danny asked for was impossible. Undoable. Ridiculous.

But...I had a few days of getting on Santa's naughty list, of me enjoying the company of two Greek gods, and just like they teased me endlessly, maybe I ought to do the same to them.

I couldn't believe I was even entertaining the idea.

I lifted my chin, swallowed back the trepidation, and smiled. "I promise you'll be dreaming about me for months after this."

That time, it was Danny's mouth that dropped open. I just offered them both a smirk as I sauntered toward my bedroom.

NAUGHTY LIST #5: GIVING TWO HOTTIES A SHOW

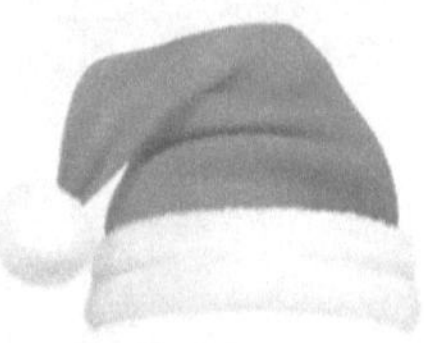

My heart was beating a million miles an hour. Why had I agreed to this again?

"You should undress first. Only fair. I was completely naked when you saw me. I wanna see all your clothes on the floor," Danny demanded as he and Max carried in a chair each into my bedroom. Danny must have caught Max up on what was happening.

They placed them near the door to get a nice side view of my bed where I lay.

Well, technically I laid under the blanket fully clothed, shaking with excitement that I was doing this, proud of myself for not wimping out.

I unzipped my jeans, then wriggled out of them and my underwear, all in the privacy of my blanket.

I pushed them out from under the blanket and they fell near the bed, the guys' eyes bulging at the sight.

"And the top," Max contributed.

"This isn't a burlesque show, you know," I snapped.

"No, it's an you-owe-me-for-spying-on-me event." Danny folded his arms over his stomach, sitting there with his legs wide, slouched on the chair and looking so gorgeous, while Max leaned forward, elbows on his thighs, the intensity behind his gaze mesmerizing.

Stiffening, I popped my head up from the pillow. "I was not spying. You left the door open. You wanted me to see you. Bet that's why you used my lotion."

He rubbed his hands together. "Yep, all part of my big plan to watch you tickle yourself under a blanket."

"Blanket needs to go." Max was on his feet.

I froze and clutched them to my chest. "Don't touch them. We need rules."

He cocked an eyebrow and sat back down.

"First, you can't touch the bed. Second, you can't take the blanket off me. Three..." I tried frantically to think of another point. "You can't leave your seats."

They both glanced at each other and got to their feet, holding the seats to their asses and moved a few steps closer before sitting back down.

"Ha ha, very funny." I raised my eyebrows at them.

"Time is ticking," Max said, tapping his wrist with no watch.

"You can't rush this. I need to get in the mood."

Danny ripped his shirt off in an instant and smirked. "I can remove my pants too if it helps."

"No, no, all good." I was burning up with heat under here, already pulsing with desire. It felt like all the air had been sucked from the room.

I looked over at them both, waiting, and their looks could make a nun drop her panties. I had no control over the effect they had on me.

For so long I'd always played it safe and been the good girl. I might never see these guys again, and this was a Christmas I'd never forget. I embraced the bravery surging through me, not wanting to regret this chance to just be wild, do something different, and for a chance, not to be me.

Ducking under the blanket, I shuffled out of my top and bra, and slid them out of bed. When I peeked out over the top of the blanket, both guys stared at me like wolves. A flash of something dark and burning hot lashed over their eyes. I was the bunny they were about to pounce on, that was clear.

My breath went still in my lungs while my body flooded with arousal.

I offered them a smirk and slid my hands to my breasts and squeezed, the blanket thin enough that it revealed my movements. There were butterflies in the pit of my stomach as I watched their eyes follow my every move.

Pushing a hand down my stomach, my fingers slid lower and I spread my legs.

Danny shifted in his seat, adjusting the front of his pants, and I was barely catching my breath that I was actually doing this.

"You know we could lend a helping hand, if you'd like?" Danny asked, while Max sat there silent and still, completely captivated by me. There was a power I held over the men in that moment, a power where they'd do anything I asked them right now.

I grinned back at them, pushing my fingers deeper. I was so incredibly wet.

I'd never met anyone like them. Anyone who could turn

me on with their voices alone, with the things they said, who got me so heated up.

I inhaled my heated scent, and at once I seemed to feel everything. The blanket pressing down on me like a lover laying over me, the air in the room, the quickened breathing from the two men watching me, their anticipation.

My heart was racing, and I thought about their hands running all over me. My finger worked over the silkiness between my legs, and I closed my eyes as the desire built inside me.

Again, I pictured both of the men with me. Danny kissing me hard, his fingers finding my puckered nipples, squeezing them, and I moaned, loving the pain and pleasure it erupted within me. Max would climb onto the bed and push my legs wider. He was so much bigger than I expected, and his cock was hot and thick between us.

Shivers raced over my flesh, and the faster I stroked, the closer I pushed myself to the edge, the more I imagined Max's fingers flowing down between my legs, finding my wetness.

I arched my hips to meet him. But he never pushed into me, not yet. He just teased me with his fingers running up and down my opening as he watched my reaction.

I moaned and my body was burning up, faster and hotter. I imagined Danny taking a nipple into his mouth and Max lifting my hips off the bed, pulling me higher, his face between my thighs. His tongue flicked out, licking me, making a delicious sound. His mouth sealed over me, sucking me, his teeth grazing my clit... *Oh, fudgeee.*

Then everything erupted. Fire exploded within me, pleasure pulsed deep and real, shuddering through me. A cry spilled past my lips as I clenched my thighs, euphoria crashing over me in a brutal rhythm affecting every inch of my body.

"Holy shit!" Danny murmured, and I opened my eyes, laying under the blanket, sprawled like I'd had the best orgasm ever.

Both guys were watching me, gasping, their chests working each rushed breath. Danny had his hand on his groin, while Max swallowed loudly.

"That was the sexiest fucking thing I've ever seen," Max admitted.

Danny jumped up and stormed out of the room, his footsteps fading until I heard the bathroom door shut.

Max was standing now, the smoldering intensity on his face begged me to peel the sheets off myself, to ask him to join me. But I didn't. Couldn't. Wouldn't.

"You might have just broken us," he said. "And you are getting super close to being on Santa's naughty list."

NAUGHTY LIST # 6: DOING IT IN PUBLIC

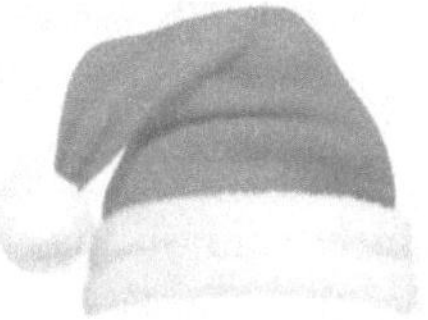

"I'm bored," were the first words out of Danny's mouth when I came out of my room the next morning. Danny was slumped in front of the TV, nursing a cup of coffee. "Could definitely go another round of last night." He winked at me.

I blushed almost instantly and changed the topic, still unable to believe what I'd done last night. Max's words stayed with me, twisting through me all night that I had such an effect on them.

You might have just broken us.

But I couldn't let myself believe it meant anything more than two guys enjoying a show. I mean, I was under the blanket the whole time.

"Where's Max?" I asked, looking around for a sign of

him. Just from the few days we spent together, I had noticed that Max was an early riser.

"He's at the gym. He probably will be there for hours judging by his terrible attitude this morning about all the "shit" he had been putting in his body the last few days," Danny said with a smirk, leaning back against the couch and putting his arms behind his head. I couldn't help but salivate over the gorgeous lines of his muscles in that position.

"Didn't feel like going with him?" I asked.

He pulled an arm from behind his head and flexed it. "Does it look like I need to?" he responded.

I couldn't help but laugh at his ridiculousness. Both he and Max had the kind of bodies that looked like they required hours at the gym to maintain, something I certainly had never had the patience for.

"Let's go out," Danny said suddenly, hopping up from the couch. "Before I fall to my knees and beg you for a repeat of last night."

I snorted when I got the full view of him, totally ignoring his comment. He was wearing pajama pants covered in pictures of elves and the bottom of his shirt said, "I sleigh." His bad boy looks and tattoos clashed deliciously with his festive attire and his playful personality as a whole.

"What? Don't like fashion?" he asked proudly as he showcased his getup.

"I'm going to go change and then we can go somewhere. But should we wait for Max?" I responded as I began to walk back to my room.

"Nawwww. Like I said, he'll be awhile. He can meet up with us later. And besides, I wouldn't mind some alone time with you," he said with a waggle of his eyebrows.

I couldn't prevent my face from blushing as I thought

again about what I had done in front of him and Max last night. I rushed to my room before he could see my flushed face. Judging by his laughter that followed me, he was well aware of what I had been thinking about.

Twenty minutes later we were on our way out of the hotel. We stopped by a Starbucks so I could get another white chocolate peppermint mocha (since I was addicted) and a pumpkin muffin, and then we set off again for Michigan Avenue.

It was freezing again today but between my mocha and Danny's arm around my waist, I felt pretty warm as we walked.

We were almost to the Nordstrom's entrance when Danny stopped abruptly on the sidewalk and pointed to some mistletoe that was attached to the entryway of the store. "I think we better kiss, Belle. I've heard it's bad luck to ignore mistletoe," he said in a serious tone that was belied by the twinkle in his eye.

I froze. I mean, what I had done last night was way beyond a kiss. But still…it felt like once I opened this gate, I wasn't going to be able to stop myself from blowing it wide open and doing much…much…more.

"Just a little kiss," said Danny. "It's mistletoe. It would be a tragedy if we didn't take advantage of it," he reasoned.

It wasn't really that crazy that this would be the next step after last night. This whole escape from reality still seemed unreal though. This was something that would happen to Myles, not to me. But it *was* happening to me.

Before I could stop myself, I grabbed Danny's shirt in my hands and gave him the best kiss I could muster.

His lips were firm and hot against mine. If he was surprised by my sudden movement, he didn't dwell on it, immediately taking charge of the kiss. His arms went around my waist, pulling me flush against him as he ran his tongue along the seam of my lips. Delicious.

I could feel his muscles flex beneath my hands, which I had uncurled, spreading my fingers across his chest as he deepened the kiss. His tongue tangled with mine and his other hand slid downward, cupping my butt and hauling me even tighter against his body.

It was without a doubt the best kiss I'd ever had in my life and I couldn't get enough. He tasted like coffee and cinnamon, his tongue taking control of my mouth. I decided right then and there that, screw my white chocolate mocha, these were my new favorite flavors.

He knew exactly what he wanted, and I was more than happy to give it to him. I had never felt so desired...the evidence of this pressing hard against my stomach. Arching against him, I felt him groan and it gave me the courage to keep going. I slid my hands upward, twisting in his soft hair, wanting whatever he would give me.

Through the haze of desire, I heard a throat clear behind us. We broke apart. A shopper was standing there with an annoyed look on her face, waiting to go through the store's entrance that we were currently blocking.

I felt my face go red, and I crossed my arms over my chest, staring down at the sidewalk as if I had been caught doing something bad. Which, technically, I probably had been. Or had been about to be doing.

"Sorry about that, ma'am. Just taking advantage of the holiday season," smirked Danny, as he stepped aside with a bow to let her in. Of course, she wasn't immune to his charms and walked through the door with a huge smile on her face.

Danny pushed me through the door after her, his hands on my waist. As soon as we were in the store, he pressed a kiss on my neck before letting me go. "I've been wanting to do that since the moment I saw you," he whispered in my ear.

"Why didn't you do it then?" I taunted him, surprising both of us. I walked quickly away. After a second, where I'm pretty sure I had left him dazed and confused...he caught up with me.

We managed to spend the next hour in and out of stores at the mall that Nordstrom was connected to...but I couldn't tell you what I saw. Danny was too distracting. That kiss seemed to have lit a fire in both of us and we couldn't keep our hands off of each other.

After another quick kiss, after an hour of ones just like that, Danny groaned and grabbed my hand, dragging me through the mall with determined strides.

"Where are we going?" I yelped, as I tried to keep up with him.

We turned a corner, and both stopped in surprise. In front of us must have been the mall's Santa Claus exhibit. This was way more elaborate than I had seen in other malls however as they had set up a whole house for kids to visit Santa that resembled a gingerbread house. It evidently hadn't opened for business yet based on the fact that the windows and doors were closed and the sign next to the house said operating hours were from twelve pm to five pm.

Danny walked up to the house and tried the door, giving a small 'whoop' when it opened up. Before I could say anything, he then dragged me straight into the little cottage, closing the door after us. He pushed me against one of the walls, that I was grateful appeared to be sturdy enough to support my weight.

"It was a bit crowded out there, don't you think?" he asked with a naughty grin.

I tried to arrange my features into a neutral reaction like I wasn't having heart palpitations at our proximity and location. "You're right," I said with a hopefully serious nod. "Very, very busy." He swept my hair back off my shoulder and I thought I was going to melt. He kissed my throat next and now I was shivering. "It's going to open soon. Santa and his elves could be here any minute," I managed to get out even though it was hard to form words at the moment.

He pressed his lips just beneath my ear. "Mmhmm," he responded. "That's true. Should I stop?" he asked as he kissed down my neck. My body arched against him.

"Probably," I murmured.

He raised his neck to look at me. "I'll make it quick," he countered, and then before I could argue, he brought his mouth down hard against mine.

My knees went weak as I was pressed for the first time in my life firmly between a wall and a hard body. A very hard body.

I wrapped my arms around his neck as he pressed his mouth against mine, easing my lips open so his tongue was tangled with mine. He tasted so dang good. Heat rushed through my body, pooling between my legs, my skin tingling as he ran his hands up my arms to cup my face. He deepened the kiss, his fingers tight in my hair. I couldn't get enough, my own hands roaming eagerly across his wide, muscular chest and broad shoulders, wishing that there wasn't a sweater between us. Wishing that there wasn't anything between us.

I wanted him. I arched against him, wanting to be closer, wanting more. He groaned as I rocked my hips forward, responding by pinning me more firmly to the wall, dragging my hands up above my head, our fingers linked. He pressed his pelvis against mine and I could feel exactly how much he wanted me, his desire hard against my stomach. I shuddered, knowing that he felt this too. That I was making him feel this way. It was intoxicating, and I couldn't get enough. Tearing his mouth from mine, he began to drop hot, seductive kisses down the side of my throat. Keeping my hands pinned with one of his, he brought the other one down to my hips. It began to inch upward while his mouth came lower until they met at my breast.

I moaned as his tongue circled my breast through the fabric of my bra and shirt. My jacket was off already. I had torn it off I guess when he had first started to kiss me.

I thrust my chest forward, and as if he had read my mind, Danny pulled down the neckline of my shirt and the lace cup of my bra with one smooth gesture, his hot mouth closing over my breast immediately. My head fell back against the wall as his tongue sent sensations zinging through me. He was so good at this.

With my hands still pinned, all I could do to bring him closer was wrap my leg around the back of his, pulling the hard ridge of his cock between my thighs. I felt him smile against my breast, and without missing a beat, his hand slid down my side, down my leg, hooking my knee more firmly around him. He released my hands to cup my butt with his other hand, yanking me up against him, trapping my upper body between him and the wall, both of my legs wrapped around his waist. "Fuck," he groaned against my mouth as our bodies aligned. Unable to help myself, I tilted my hips, bringing him even closer, my fingers digging into his shoulders as heat built inside of me. I was desperate for release. Desperate for him. I kissed him, without any finesse, without any restraint. I put everything I had into that kiss, forgetting reality, forgetting everything. All that mattered was Danny. Danny and me. I wanted him. All of him.

He ripped himself away from me and we both just stared at each other. Not a half a second passed however before we were tearing each other's clothes off. His sweater was gone in a flash. My shirt was yanked off, the straps of my bra sliding down my arms. I fumbled with Danny's belt, feeling him groan against my mouth each time my fingers brushed against his cock, straining against his zipper.

Finally, unable to get him free, I pulled back. "Lose your pants," I ordered, out of breath.

I was full of adrenaline and lust and couldn't wait to discover every last inch of him. His blue eyes were on fire as he took a step back, his gaze never leaving mine as he undid his belt effortlessly, and then with a single smooth movement, removed his pants and briefs, leaving him beautifully naked in front of me. I blinked.

Holy sleigh bells, every time I saw his naked chest, it caught me by surprise. They really should sculpt this guy from marble and put him in a museum. His chest heaved. He was hard... and ready. So was I. Desire pulsed through me, but I stood there, completely lost in my appreciative examination of his body. With a grin, Danny stepped forward, and somehow got my jeans off, leaving me there in just my thong.

"You're perfect," he murmured, his eyes screaming with want.

I flushed...everywhere. Feeling timid under his scrutiny, I slowly hooked my thumbs into the waistband of my thong and slid them down my thighs, suddenly well aware I was naked inside of Santa's house in a mall.

"Gorgeous," he murmured as he touched a hand to my cheek, the gesture so gentle and sweet that it made my heart do a flip in my chest.

"Come here." He didn't have to repeat himself. I

wrapped my arms around his neck and pulled myself against him, finally feeling the heat of his naked body against mine. Without warning, I was hoisted up into his arms, his hands on my ass, legs wrapped around him.

He was hot and hard where I was wet and aching for him. He kissed my neck and the curve of my shoulder, alternating open-mouth kisses and sharp little nips. My entire body was tingling with anticipation, my skin humming. His hands roamed up and down my curves, his words and fingers worshipping them.

"These are perfection," he declared, pressing a hot kiss against the slope of my breast. Pleasure shot through me.

"I want you," I breathed, sounding husky, even to myself.

He groaned and began to pour attention on my stomach, my belly button, my hip bones, beginning to sink to his knees as he did so.

I was pretty sure I was going to spontaneously explode if he wasn't inside of me soon. It had never been this way before. I had never, in my very limited experience, wanted someone so bad that I would have begged for relief.

I reached down between us and wrapped my fingers around Danny's cock. His descent stilled immediately as he pressed his forehead against my belly.

I began to stroke him wondering how I had suddenly become this wanton creature.

He felt incredible, and I loved the way he groaned as my hand moved. I had barely begun to explore before I found my hands pinned above my head.

"You keep that up, and this will be over in about a second," he told me with a grin. "And I want to be inside you when I come."

"I want that too," I gasped, watching his gaze go even hotter. "Please? Now?"

He let me down and crouched down to his jean's pocket where he pulled out a foil packet. I watched, anticipation coursing through me, as he ripped it open and rolled the condom on. The image of his hand stroking his cock turned me on even more, something he must have noticed because he stroked himself once more, only slower. I bit my lip, and this time he groaned.

He gave me a wicked grin and then began to stroke me, his touch light at first, so light that it offered no relief. I tilted my hips towards him, eager for more, and he gave it to me, his wet fingers circling my clit. Heat built in my core, my entire body going tense as he slid one finger inside of me, and then another. I was so close, so ready, my head pressed against the wall, my skin hot as he stroked me harder and faster. And just as my climax was cresting, he released my hands. I fisted them beside me, moaning, with my breath shallow, my hips straining for release.

Danny replaced his hand with his cock and in one smooth thrust, was inside of me just as my orgasm shattered through me, my body arching off the wall. Holy crap. I was reeling, but Danny hadn't even gotten started yet. He held himself still until I returned to earth and then, as the after-shocks faded, began to move inside me. I had never been a girl who was capable of orgasms during sex, but within a few moments, as Danny tilted my hips, hitting my clit just right, I knew that was going to change.

"You feel so fucking good," he groaned, his fingers digging into my hips.

I kissed him, thrusting my tongue into his mouth, matching his rhythm. Even though I had already come, I was greedy for more. I wanted him deeper. Wrapping my legs around him, I made us both gasp from the new angle, the new sensations. My body began to tighten as I felt another orgasm rushing towards me. What was this guy doing to me?

Danny's thrusts became faster, more frantic, and I knew he was close too. The pleasure spiraled higher, and I dug my fingers into his arms, urging him on, my moans drowning out any other sounds, the two of us lost in a haze of pleasure and intensity. Here it came again. Yes. My toes curled as another orgasm overcame me, my voice hoarse as I cried out. Danny thrust once, twice, and then found his release, his strong body shaking as he came, our naked bodies collapsing against the wall.

"Thanks for being Santa's helper and holding my sack," Danny suddenly said with a snort as he lifted his head from my neck to look at me.

"Oh my gosh." I all but shrieked in laughter as he pulled out and set me down.

Suddenly, a noise came from outside, reminding us of where we were. Panicked, we threw on our clothes. Once we were dressed, Danny opened the door of the cottage a crack, and peered outside. "It's just an elf. Santa isn't here yet," he whispered as if it wasn't a big deal that we were going to walk out of the house in front of a mall employee who was probably going to call security on us, if he or she hadn't already.

Looking perfectly at ease, if a bit sweaty from our romp, he grabbed my hand and pulled me out of the house. The worker, who was indeed dressed as an elf, just looked at us shocked as we walked past her. Danny shot her a wink before we sped up and turned the corner back into the main artery of the mall.

"I can't believe that just happened," I said with a laugh.

"Probably happens all the time. People get frisky around

the holidays," Danny replied jokingly as he pulled out his phone.

"It's Max. He's wondering where we are. Should I have him meet us for lunch?" he asked as he read a text on his phone.

My stomach trembled at the thought of seeing Max so soon after what just happened. "Sure," I responded in a choked voice.

Danny gave me a knowing grin as he typed back a response to Max.

"Hmmm. Looks like it's just us until later. Max has a meeting he has to take online."

"A meeting?"

"Yep, just something for school," Danny said vaguely.

I couldn't help but feel like he was being intentionally vague, but I didn't push him. Despite the fact that we had just gotten *very* intimate with one another, we were still basically strangers.

Which is what I wanted when I started all of this...

Right?

NAUGHTY LIST #7: RELENTLESS TEASING

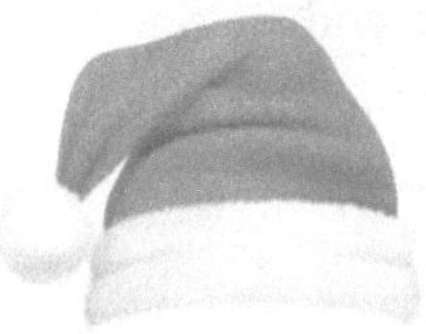

"Where are we going?" I asked as Danny and I walked down the sidewalk, my hand in his. The afternoon was already dark with clouds and snow coming down in thick patches. After lunch we had done more window shopping and wandered over to the Cloud Gate exhibit or "The Bean" as Danny and everyone else seemed to call it, to take goofy pictures in the giant sculpture.

"Max is meeting us at an ice bar not far from our hotel. We're gonna have a few early drinks before dinner." He glanced over at me when he spoke and drew me closer to avoid a man walking straight into me.

The ground grew slippery under my boots, and Danny held me close so I didn't fall.

The place we entered was dark and lit up with Christmas lights. An enormous, fake polar bear stood in the corner on its hind legs, a leather chair near him. The walls were made of metal with giant bolts looking like we'd stepped into a steampunk world.

"Wow, this is a bar?" I asked, glancing around at the small counter where Max was speaking to an older woman and handing over his credit card. Steampunk goggles hung off hooks on the wall along with fake laser guns. This had to be the strangest place I'd visited.

"You've never been to an ice bar?" Danny asked, curiously.

I shook my head just as the lady waved us over to join her and Max at the end of the counter and we headed toward them. She handed me a lush faux fur coat the color of snow that easily fell to my knees. "Put this on then I'll take you into the bar."

"It's going to be that cold in there?" I slipped my arms into the sleeves and pulled the lush, warm coat around myself, the fur tickling my jaw.

Danny wore a black one, and with his size, he reminded me of a black bear, while Max's was a tanned color and could easily pass for a grizzly. We were each next given a set of black gloves.

"Keep these on at all times," the woman instructed. "Inside, nearly everything is made of ice. There are cameras around the room with buttons nearby on the walls to take photos of yourselves. No other photos are allowed to be taken."

"Okay," I said, completely unsure of what to expect, but I was bouncing in my boots with curiosity.

We followed her to a round metal door that she pulled open and walked into a dark corridor before she opened another door in front of us, and a new world opened up before me.

I stepped into a room completely covered in ice, the walls, the sculptures of more bears, a throne, tables and stools, an air hockey table, and even a board game of chess. Everything made of ice. Fur pelts covered the seats, and the deeper I stepped into this frozen wonderland, the quicker the cold snapped around me.

"I love this place," I cooed, turning on the spot, mesmerized, unable to believe I never knew this type of bar existed.

"What would you like to drink, gorgeous?" Danny asked, his hand slipping into mine, our fingers intertwined, and he led me to the long ice bar where several other people were ordering.

Max handed me a menu and I scanned it. "Zombie Tiki cocktail please. The rum will warm me up."

Danny dragged me into his arms, his lips on my head. "I'll keep you warm."

I pressed against him, adoring his warmth, feeling like somehow this was normal. Me with these guys, going out and enjoying ourselves like nothing in the world could touch us. And staring into his eyes, all I could think about was our early time in Santa's little workshop. I should be embarrassed about what we had done, but I wouldn't change a thing about that moment.

We got our cocktails, and I looked around and eyed the free air hockey table.

"Let's play," Max said, waiting at one end of the table, glancing at me with a challenge in his eyes.

Another gulp of my delicious rum and orange drink, and Danny took my glass.

I jumped in and gripped my mallet. "Let's go, grizzly," I teased.

He cocked a brow, his lips curling upward so adorably, I almost wanted to crawl over the ice table and steal a kiss. "Best of three games," he said and leaned closer, his voice lowering. "If I win, you give Danny and I a repeat of last night, but this time no blanket and we're allowed to touch, and if you win..." His gaze drifted to the ceiling, prodding his chin with his index finger.

"You'll do a strip dance for me," I blurted, finding my bravery, and my whole body buzzed.

"I love where this is going," Danny muttered, eyeing me with those hypnotizing eyes.

"Deal!" Max answered so fast, I started thinking I should have asked for more.

He placed the puck on the line in front of him and attacked.

Reflexes kicked in, and I defended my goal post, focused on winning and beating him at his own game.

"I can't wait to see your dance." I wacked the puck so hard it slid right past his hand and shot right into the goal post.

"Yes!" I jumped up and down on the spot, while the boys narrowed their eyes at me.

"Max, you better not lose, man, seriously," Danny warned.

I couldn't stop laughing and took another drink of my cocktail, shook myself, and I faced Max.

"Let's do this, Perky," he started.

"Playing dirty, I see." I cracked my knuckles and grabbed my weapon and we were off. That time, Danny was cheering and drinking my cocktail.

Just as I looked over at him to protest him drinking all of my drink, Max smashed the puck past my defenses and shot a goal.

He exploded with a cheer so loud that it gained the attention of others from the bar, getting people to come and watch us.

Sweat rolled down my back. Yep, nothing like pressure, but I wouldn't let him win. Not when I could see that delicious body as he stripped for me personally.

I straightened my shoulders and glared at Max. "You're going down."

He half snickered. "Babe, I'd love to."

His words took me off guard and he dove in, shooting the puck. Abruptly, I dove down and defended my side and fought back. "Dirty cheat," I muttered.

The final round went on and on, both of us intense, nothing was distracting me, and the crowds around us fell silent... too silent.

Max swung his mallet so hard; it sent the puck flying off the table, past ducking heads and hit a bear statue.

I burst out laughing as Danny chased after it. "You want to win this badly, don't you?"

He dragged a gloved hand over his lower lip, and my attention caught on his full mouth and how much I'd love to feel it against mine.

"You have no idea," he replied sexily, his captivating mouth drawing the attention of more than just me.

Two girls dolled up approached him, laughing, one of them reaching over to touch his arm, drawing his attention from me.

I couldn't make out their whispers, but both were gawking at him like he was a superstar. And it burned me up on the inside to see them touching his arm through the fur coat, to think it was okay to hit on him when he was clearly in a game with me... he could be with me for all they knew. Heat lashed over my chest just as Danny sidled up against me, placing the puck down in front of me.

"You give me what I want, and I'll give you what you want." His breath washed over my ear, sending warmth over my body.

I looked over to see him staring at me, then at a distracted Max with the girls who wouldn't leave him alone. "Oh, you're devious," I whispered back to Danny.

"For you, hell yeah. Do it, babe," he urged.

I turned, the giggles infuriating me, and I wanted to drive the puck into the blonde to get her to leave Max alone. I readied my mallet.

"And go!" Danny called out.

I whacked my mallet into the puck just as Max swung around. His eyes widened, his hand jutting out to stop my assault, but he was too damn slow, and I struck the goal.

"Oh, yeah!" I shouted and jumped up and down with Danny by my side, while Max glared at us both.

"Keep your eye on the game," Danny teased.

Max strolled away from those flirting girls and approached me, stretching out his hand in a friendly shake of congratulations.

I tilted my head up and accepted, but he drew me closer to him in a heartbeat, his warm breath on my face, a hand on my cheek, and my heart was thundering.

"Very clever, though I might think you were jealous of those girls. Were you jealous, Belle?"

I rolled my eyes, hiding how angry I was that they had flirted with him right in front of me. "I don't know what you're talking about."

"They mean nothing to me. I only have eyes for you." He pushed a lock of blond hair out of my face and ran his thumb over my lower lip. All I could think about was what he would taste like if he just came a little closer...about how he felt against me.

He leaned in closer as if sensing my unease, his lips finally grazing mine. Unable to hold back, I pushed myself closer, up on tippy toes to reach him easily. He was soft and tender, tasting like vodka and sex, and I kissed him back, gripping his fur coat to keep him close to me. Maybe I was selfish for wanting him all to myself, for wanting both men and not willing to share them with any other girls.

Danny's hand was at my lower back, and I pulled back, falling against his chest, his arms around my shoulders. When I looked back at the air-hockey table, both girls glared at me, looking ready to claw out my eyes.

"Okay, time for more drinks." Max's voice drew my attention.

"Yes. Let's have a jingle ball tonight!" Danny added, and I laughed at his silliness.

For the next twenty minutes we sat at an ice table on fur pelts and laughed, each making up the worst puns and downing drinks.

"I'm pretty sure I've lost feeling in my toes. They are frozen from the cold in here," I said, trying to wriggle them in my boots. "I didn't really feel the cold before, now it's spreading up my legs."

"Okay, let me grab the last drinks, and we're out of here." Max stood up and seemed to sway on his way to the bar. I couldn't remember how many cocktails we'd had so far, even my head swayed.

My phone beeped, and I pulled it out of my pocket to see a message from Todd. I cringed on the inside and made the mistake of opening it.

Missing you, sis. Are you missing me?

I almost gagged and hastily tucked my phone away,

hating him for almost ruining my buzz. I looked up only to find the earlier brunette near Max at the bar, draping herself all over him. Danny was with them, placing our order instead, while Max tried to pull away from the girl who wouldn't leave him alone.

It was embarrassing for her how desperate she was acting. Still, I seethed at seeing her with them. Maybe I'd had too much to drink, or I couldn't get my lips to stop tingling from my kiss with Max, to stop burning up at the memory of me with Danny in the elf house, but they were mine, even if only for this short time in Chicago. They'd grown on me and I wasn't ready to let them go.

The desperado was now pushing her breasts against Max's arm, leaning in like she might kiss him, her hand splayed all over his chest.

Max shook his head and gently pushed her aside.

I was on my feet before I knew it, marching closer, and the icy room was swaying around me, my whole body buzzing from too much alcohol.

Danny handed me my cocktail in a v-shaped glass, when the brunette stepped into my face, spitting her threat. "Slut. Who do you think you are?"

My hackles bristled, and I'd had enough of her. "They aren't interested in you, get over it."

I turned away, but she snatched my arm, squeezing.

Anger raged, and I turned, tossing my drink into her face. I then ripped my arm out of her grip.

She cried out, her eyes round discs, and she drew everyone's attention.

Danny was at my side, prying the glass from my fingers before placing it on the counter. Drinking his cocktail in record time, he wrapped an arm around my back, Max on my other side, and we rushed for the door.

"Let's get out of here my little hellcat," Danny murmured, and once outside in the reception room, we removed our fur coats and handed them to the lady before we made haste out of there.

I couldn't stop laughing. "I can't believe I just did that. But she deserved it."

"I love your feistiness," Max added. "That girl was so clingy, and it was fucking annoying."

"She didn't understand boundaries or that you were there with me."

Max looked over at me, his eyes smiling. "I like the sound of that last part."

Danny tightened his arm around my waist as we hurried through the worsening storm and into the foyer of our hotel and whisked toward the elevator.

I stumbled inside the elevator after him. "What's the rush?"

He turned to me. "You really need to ask?"

"True," I said with a smirk. "I can't wait for Max's strip tease either."

Danny rose a brow, those magnificent blue eyes glinting beneath the lights. "Remember, I helped you win, and it wasn't to see him strip."

I fake laughed and nudged his arm. "I don't know what you're talking about. I won fair and square."

When his mouth dropped open and he reached for me, the elevator doors slid open.

I jumped out of his grasp before bolting down the corridor, giggling uncontrollably.

Danny was on my heels, pounding the carpet behind me with fast steps. His hand lashed out, snatched my arm and hauled me back to him. His eyes were filled with lust and hunger.

My feet tripped over each other, and I stumbled into him, my hands pressed to his chest, my eyes lifting to meet his ravenous ones. My heart was racing and my whole body buzzed with an exhilaration I hadn't felt in years.

Hands gripped my hips and he lifted me to stand on his feet, then walked me backward until my back hit the wall in a familiar position. He pushed himself against me, his erection nestled against my lower stomach, and I gasped. I adored how he reacted around me.

"You're in so much trouble," he grumbled, his mouth on my neck, arms sliding to my ass, groping me.

Max leaned his shoulder into the wall right next to us, and I glanced over at him. He blew me a kiss and just stared at me with so much admiration in his eyes as if I were the most beautiful thing he'd ever seen. Of course, that couldn't be true, but for those few moments, I let myself believe that it was. That by some miracle, I could have two men like them in my life.

I reached over a hand and fisted his shirt playfully. "You going to kiss me, sweet lips?"

His laughter was bewitching. Strong, deep, and hot as hell.

But instead of leaning in, he pushed off the wall and wandered down the hall. Danny lifted his head and I slid out from under him and ran after Max toward our room.

"You're such a tease," I threw over my shoulder as I marched past Max and into the room.

Danny was behind me in seconds, his arms looped around me as he lifted me off the floor.

I cried out in laughter. He carried me all the way to the couch and released me. I fell onto the cushions and rolled onto my back as both men stood there, staring down at me.

Warmth spread inside me as pleasure took hold. "So, where should we set up for the show." I eyed Max.

He was shaking his head, making a faint tsking sound that aroused me to no end. I had this impression that Max didn't let others take control of him very often.

"Come on, baby doll," Danny said. "Off the couch." He had his phone in his hand, and after a few taps, a song I recognized played. Santa Baby by Eartha Kitt with that gorgeous deep voice.

Danny flopped down next to me, patting my butt to squeeze over.

I shifted to a sitting position and sidled up to Danny, then looked over to Max standing near the fireplace in front of us.

"You ready?" I asked with a smirk.

He raised his eyebrows in a way that told me he was super ready. "Give me two shakes and I'll be right back." He darted into his bedroom, and I couldn't resist but watch the way his muscles moved under his clothes when he walked, at how tight and gorgeous his ass was. Deep breaths.

"What do you think he's doing?" I asked.

"Could be anything with him. What I want to know is if you're going to be the main act tonight?" There was hunger in his voice just as it had been earlier in the day where he couldn't get enough of me. And I desperately wanted more, but part of me was scared that I was moving so fast.

"Maybe we can order some food?" I suggested, gaining myself a cute pout from Danny.

"Fine." He pushed off the couch. "But when I come back, you're sitting on my lap."

I raised a brow he completely ignored, and I just reclined while Danny ordered food and Max was doing gosh knew what. There was something exhilarating about the general banter between us, about how everything they did and said revolved about getting closer to me. I'd never experienced this before, and I adored every moment. The planes were still grounded today, but part of me wondered if I'd eagerly head home if they weren't?

Finally, Danny leapt back on the couch with me, the cushion beneath me bouncing so hard, I jostled in my seat. I shifted in my seat and placed my legs over his lap before he dragged me up there. His hands were already on my feet, peeling off my socks, one at a time before massaging my soles and toes.

"Now this is heaven." His fingers pressed into my feet right where they were sore from walking so much.

"This fire is so cozy, the snuggle is real," he muttered while eyeing me.

"Have you memorized these puns, or do you have them written up your arm? Seriously, they are just rolling out. And they are pretty funny."

He worked my toes, stretching them, and I just moaned at how amazing it felt.

When I looked up, he was staring at me like I'd accidentally touched his dick. "What?"

"Don't moan like that. It does things to me."

And he was completely serious. "Okay, fine I'll control my moans if you tell me the deal with you and puns?"

"They're just something my dad used to always say during Christmas when I grew up, and they remind me of him at this time of the year. They kinda make me feel like he's still around. Anyway," he cleared his throat. "I don't want to talk about that now. This is a time for festivities."

My heart clenched at hearing his story, knowing there was a lot more to it than he had said. I reached over and placed a hand on his. "Well, I love them. Never stop."

"Thanks, babe." He blew me a kiss.

At once, the music from Max's phone suddenly changed to an upbeat tune, and he emerged from around the corner in his jeans and tee.

"You haven't even changed," I said. "What were you doing?"

He wriggled a finger at me and stumbled over the rug. "Just sit back and enjoy, sexy."

"You're really drunk now, aren't you," I said to him.

"Nope. Everything is just a bit fuzzy," he teased.

"Okay let's get this over with," Danny added. "Roast your chestnuts over the fire already."

I cut him a look and couldn't stop laughing at his crazy puns.

"It'd rather watch you up there," he said, bluntly.

Suddenly, the music rose in volume, and I turned my attention on the sex on legs prowling in front of us.

I moved my body to the music on the couch, adoring these guys so much. And my gaze locked on Max.

Sinful, pale eyes, messy golden hair, and tanned skin calling my name.

Completely hypnotized, I had eyes only for him and sat back ready to be entertained.

Max stood, legs wide, eyes on me, as his hand trailed down the front of his tee. His hips were doing a small sway. In slow motion, he bunched the hem of his tee and started to lift the fabric over perfect ripped abs that had me drooling, then over his chest and stayed there, revealing hard planes of muscles. He flexed one pec, then the other, and I was completely lost to him already.

"Boo," Danny cried out and tossed a small pillow at him, catching Max right in the gut.

But Max didn't seem to care and went with it, ripping off

his shirt. I pulled my lower lip between my teeth, chewing on it as I stared at the god in front of me. Biceps I could hang off. Every inch of me was tingling with a need to reach over and touch. But I held back. I mean I had some level of control. I wasn't a complete beast.

"Take it off," I cooed.

Danny moaned. "I need something stronger if I have to watch this. It's cringeworthy."

"Why don't you get up and join him then?" I teased, prodding him.

"You couldn't handle my heat, babe." He was on his feet and headed for the hotel mini bar.

I swung my attention back to the sex on a stick man who had me drooling.

"Get me a whiskey, bro," Max called out to Danny as he popped open a button on his jeans, then another.

As ashamed as I should be, I let my gaze fall to where he revealed more flesh, to where a bit of dark thatch of hair appeared. My insides melted at the sight, and warmth spread through me.

"You enjoying this, babe?" he asked, while I just nodded like a horn dog in heat.

When he reached over and ran a hand down my arm, a trail of goosebumps rose in its wake. These guys affected me like no other.

Max was doing a strange sway that had me hypnotized, something that included thrusting his pelvis outward, wearing a smirk of epic proportions before popping open another button, revealing the top of...

Oh my, I was burning up.

The music was playing loud now, and Max was grinding an invisible pole. I wasn't sure if I should laugh or join him and become that pole getting way too much of his attention.

In a heartbeat he turned away from me and pushed down his jeans, and all I could stare at were the sexiest, firmest ass cheeks that I had ever seen...well other than Danny's. He was standing completely naked with his back to me.

I froze, unsure what to do, but leaving the room right now was out of the question.

Danny burst out laughing from across the room.

"What?" I asked.

Right then, Max spun to face me, and my eyes dropped like a stone to a red and green sock covering his dick. It sat upright from his clear erection; the sock pushed all the way down to cover his two potatoes. I had laughed at my friend who called them that.

I couldn't help it and started to giggle loudly at seeing this man who was a god wearing a striped sock over his dick.

Max never batted an eye and he took my hand. I let him drag me off the couch and against his hard, toned body. His arms looped around my waist and our bodies swayed to the tune. One large hand slid to the back of my head, the other to my ass, holding me in place as he moved his face next to mine. Tender lips found the softness of my neck, and then he glided over to my mouth, taking it in a delicious embrace. I was falling for his flirting while my mind kept focusing on the erection in his sock, pressed up against my stomach.

He smelled of alcohol and a sexy muskiness. Completely intoxicating.

I could get used to this kind of attention. So much so that I returned the kiss, going deeper, pressing my tongue into his mouth. I loved the way he tasted, and I moaned against him.

"So that's the strip tease, then? Pretty lame if you ask

me," Danny said sarcastically. "You could have taken your sock off," he mocked. "Given Belle a real show."

I pulled back as Danny handed Max a glass of whiskey, no ice or coke.

"I vote for Belle to strip next," Danny teased.

"Not happening. I'm tonight's winner which means I get what I want." I flopped back on the couch. "I want a drink of our finest, sir, and a foot massage by Mr. Sock over here."

My serious face turned into a silly grin and more laughter.

Both guys jumped right on my demands, and I couldn't remember the last time I felt this adored, this special...this aroused.

NAUGHTY LIST #8: LET A STRANGER TIE YOU UP

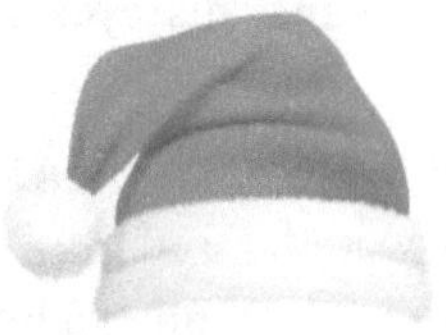

When I woke up the next morning, my mouth tasted like sandpaper and outside the window, a blizzard was engulfing the city of Chicago. I lay in bed but didn't even remember going to bed. Last thing I recalled was laughing and listening to silly puns while Max and Danny drank the mini bar dry. I must have fallen asleep on the couch and they carried me to bed.

I pushed my legs out from under the blanket and found the cold floorboards. The phone said it was past nine and I had a missed message from Todd. I sighed out loud, unable to deal with his craziness this early. So instead, I sent a quick message to my friend, Myles.

Still stuck in Chicago but having a blast. I have so much to tell you. Later.

Up on my feet, my body swayed a bit, but I was definitely more awake than last night. I grabbed clean clothes and headed to the shower, hearing no sounds from the guy's bedroom on the way. Max was probably at the gym downstairs and Danny hunting down a cafe.

After the last couple of days, I craved more time with them, and I thought that maybe it was a perfect day for going to the movies. If the weather let up a bit.

By the time I showered, dried my hair, and dressed, I wasn't surprised to find Max in the living room waiting for me. He leaned against the back of the couch, his hands deep in the pockets of his jeans, his eyes on me the second I stepped out.

"Hey gorgeous, how are you feeling today?"

"Incredible," I answered. "You?"

"Better than I expected. Danny's a bit worse for wear but he's gone to find a drug store for a headache and to pick us up loads of snacks. Storm's bad today so might be an indoor kind of day." He pushed off the couch and strolled toward me with a twinkle in his eyes.

"You look like you're up to something," I murmured with a grin on my face.

"Do I now?" he replied in a husky voice. There was something about his deep voice that drove me insane.

When he reached me, he raked his hands through my hair, pushing the loose strands off my face and kissed me. Not just a small pec, but deep and passionate, and completely knocked me off my feet with his fiery desire.

"My gosh," I breathed into his mouth. "Where did that come from?"

"Belle, I haven't been able to get you out of my mind all night. It's driving me insane, and I'm going to be honest. I want you."

I wasn't sure what to say, but words tumbled from my lips, "I want you too."

"Do you? I'm talking about the kind of want where I'll rip your clothes off and ravage you until you beg me to stop, and then I'll fuck you until you scream from two or three orgasms."

I swallowed hard, my body already humming with arousal, the heat already burning between my thighs so wildly, I was wet in a heartbeat. He'd never spoken to me this way, never said those words, and I liked it. Hell, I more than liked it. My body was trembling thinking of what he'd do to me.

"Yes," the word fell from my lips. "I want you to want me that way."

He cupped the side of my face. "You're so beautiful when you're nervous." Then he took my hand and started leading me to the bedroom.

"Now?" I asked.

His wink should be illegal, because it could convince me to do anything. He nodded. "Is that okay?"

Was it okay? My body screamed yes, and my mind... well she seemed to have gone on holiday, so I walked with him. "Completely okay."

I had no idea what to expect, but by his earlier description and promise, heck, I'll sign up for a double round.

Max led me into the bedroom that he had been sleeping in since we got here. I'm sure he could feel the shaking of my hand as we walked. Once we got into the room that resembled mine but for a color scheme of red and gold, and that it had two large beds, he stepped away from me, his gaze skimming my body, his eyes hooded by lust.

I stood with shaky legs before him. My fingers fumbled for the zipper of my dress. When I found it, I tugged the zipper down and let the dress fall away. My leggings soon followed after that.

A growl rumbled from Max and he advanced on me, lifting me up and laying me on the bed. The mattress shifted under his weight as he sat beside me. A hum of longing vibrated through my body as his hand traced my skin slowly from my neck, in between my breasts, stopping at the bottom of my stomach.

My hips writhed in his direction only to be stopped by his firm hand. "I like control in the bedroom, Belle. I don't just like it. I need it. Will you give me that?"

All I could do was take a deep breath and nod. I wanted this. Badly.

Max pulled me up, guiding my feet to the floor. A second later my bra and underwear were off, proving just how much experience he had with this kind of thing. I was pretty sure that my ex had taken five minutes of fumbling just to figure out the clasp of my bra, and he had obviously been experienced based on his activities behind my back.

Max didn't waste any time before he flipped me onto my stomach up higher on the bed. His hand softly stroked the small of my back providing me a measure of reassurance as my heart tried to leap out of my body.

"Spread your legs."

I did as he ordered, earning an approving "good girl." He lifted my arms over my head and began to wrap a silky red ribbon around my wrists, tucking and weaving it into the headboard until my feet arched. I was suspended, my toes clinging to the ground and supporting my weight. The silk brushed against my breasts as he circled my torso. He paused, and I felt a knot cinch into place between my shoulders. He crossed my stomach, coiling it just tightly enough that it dug into my flesh. His arms wrapped around me and another knot cinched across my belly button before he dropped the remaining line to swing between my spread legs.

My body molded to his movements. In that moment, he could do whatever he wanted with me and I would have been helpless. Ribbon coiled around my left ankle, pulling tightly, as he tugged it to secure it to the rest of the ribbon on my body. He repeated the action on my right ankle, spreading my legs further and further. My body ached, drawn wide. It was exhilarating, the slight pain of my bindings giving way to arousal. I hadn't been sure I could do this, but with each passing second, my body relaxed into the tension. For a moment, neither of us moved and I focused on his ragged breath.

"You're like a dream, Belle. Like a decadent gift that's designed to fulfill my every wish."

I felt him kiss my shoulder before he stepped away. The sharp metallic click of a belt unfastening alerted me to the fact that he was undressing. I itched to be able to turn my head and see him. My body tightened up as I wondered what he was going to do next. Fabric thudded softly to the floor and then his heat radiated against my vulnerable skin. I wanted to press against him, and I pulled against my elaborate bindings.

"Relax," he ordered, as he suddenly licked down my lengthened spine sending tremors through my whole body. "I'm only here to give you pleasure, my Belle. And even though it seems like I have all the power right now, the truth is that you do. Anytime you want me to stop. Anytime you don't like something I'm doing. You just tell me, and it will all stop. Do you understand?"

I nodded, but he caught my hair and stopped the movement.

"Say the words."

"I understand," I whispered, so turned on that it was hard to speak.

"What are you thinking right now?" he asked suddenly as he loosened his grip on my hair and sank his teeth into my shoulder. I groaned, as pangs of pleasure shot through me, hardening my nipples against the coolness of the room. I was flooded with sensations overwhelmed with his touch, the tone of his voice, the way his words seemed to wrap around me. I had never thought I would like something like his. But the truth was, I loved it.

Tell me," he repeated firmly as he pinched my nipple between his fingers. He twisted it, overwhelming my already saturated nerves.

"I want this more than anything," I finally breathed.

"We're just getting started," he murmured. "Seeing you wrapped up like this, completely at my will—do you have any idea what it makes me want to do to you?"

He moved off of me for a moment and I took the time to look at the bindings. The elegant knots were so intricate that I wondered how many times he'd done this before. Who else had been lucky enough to be under his control like this? A harsh wave of jealousy ripped through me and I had to push thoughts of how many other women he had done this to out of my head.

Max stepped over to the side of me, his eyes devouring me as he traced them along my body. I devoured the sight of his golden body that looked like it had been carved by the gods. I almost choked when I saw how hard he was.

Heat flushed my cheeks as I continued to stare at him. I realized that unlike how I usually felt whenever anyone paid me any attention at all, much less saw me naked, I wasn't embarrassed. I was on fire.

"The way your cheeks are flushed makes me itch to see your other cheeks pink." His words fell over me and I almost groaned at the thought. He returned to stand behind me, and I longed to feel him against me. He chuckled at my pitiful attempts to move. His palm stroked the curve of my ass before it flew against it playfully. Max rubbed the spot before delivering another smack. He repeated the gesture, spanking and caressing away the sting until my bottom stung with heat.

"Perfection." His tongue traced the edge of my ear. "Do you know why I've been obsessed with the thought of tying you up since I met you?"

I shook my head as I gasped in air.

"Because I couldn't wait to tear down that prim and proper mask you wear and see just how you look with your walls down. I could see inside of you, to that part of you that is constantly clinging to the edge, waiting greedily for someone like me to wake you up. It's happening today. Your body won't be able to fight me when I want it to come. I'm going to show you just what you do to me. I'm going to make you scream and cry and claw at that ribbon as you fall apart...and then I'm going to start all over again."

A whimper escaped my lips as he dropped between my legs. His knees hit the floor, muffled by the decadent carpet floor and I did indeed begin to struggle against my bindings as I anticipated what was about to come next.

He suddenly cupped me in his palm as his teeth nipped playfully at my sore cheeks. Then his hands parted me roughly. I barely had time to process this before his tongue plunged inside me. He sucked on me with his mouth until my knees tried to buckle, but the restraints held tight. The sudden weakness in my legs shifted more of my weight onto my arms and I screamed, unraveling on Max's talented tongue. He continued to lick me even as I cried for him to stop. I couldn't find my center, dangling between agony and elation. But just as my core began to clench, he pulled away.

I had never had someone do that to me before. And certainly not from this angle...with that amount of ferocity.

"I'm not done with you," he said wickedly as he disappeared from sight and I heard the telltale sound of foil as he got a condom.

I was lost to my role, overwhelmed by the scene unfolding around me, but starved to submit to his demands at the same time. He'd turned me into a desperate creature, and I loved it. How was I ever going to come back from this...come back from them?

My mind flashed to Danny just then, and what he had done to my body. I realized that both of them had fulfilled a secret desire I had. I needed the freedom that Danny's playful style gave me the same as I needed Max's domination. I wasn't sure how that worked, but I knew that I needed more, more, more of it all.

Max fisted my hair in his hand and turned my head, forcing me to kiss him. My mouth opened up, immediately obeying him as his tongue stroked against mine.

Suddenly, he thrust forward until he was sheathed tightly inside of me. A gasp escaped me as he teased me with the promise of fulfillment, not moving at all. His kiss deepened in response, his tongue invaded my mouth, capturing it and sucking more moans from me. He needed to start moving and end the delicious agony coursing through my body. But Max took his time as his hips slowly began to move in circles inside of me, his thickness rubbing against my throbbing clit.

"Please," I whimpered, and Max finally pulled away from my lips. He pulled out quickly and flipped me over onto my back so that my arms were crossed over my head, my legs spread, and I could look at him without discomfort. Not wasting a moment, he pushed inside of me again, not breaking our gaze, and I arched against him into the exquisite fullness I desperately sought. My body made precious contact with his hard muscles, my nipples brushing against his chest and tightening to beads. His hand slid under my back, supporting me as he rocked me towards what I knew was going to be an explosion of pleasure.

His gaze bore into me like a dare, and I couldn't look away, even as my body tightened, chasing the rapture that I knew was waiting for me.

"Say my name," he commanded suddenly.

"Max," I gasped, breathing hard as he continued to move in and out of me. I pulled on the ribbon, desperate to pull him closer, to make him mine.

"Again," he ordered as his hands slid to my hips, pinning me to him as he drove into me with relentless strokes.

"Max," I screamed as my orgasm splintered through me in violent waves that spasmed through my limbs. My eyes stayed trained on him though. He continued his thrusts, hard and fast, as he raced toward his own. Max's hands clenched my hips, and his gaze smoldered into me as he came. He was in total control, but I could feel my own slipping away with each second his skin was on mine.

He wrapped his arms around me and collapsed onto the bed, holding me close to him. I was too stunned to move, so I focused on my breathing, trying to calm my racing heart. That didn't seem possible with him still so near to me, and when he pressed a kiss to my forehead, an ache burst through my chest.

I asked myself again as I came down from what had seemed like an impossible high...how was I going to recover from this after all was said and done?

It was so much better on the naughty list.

NAUGHTY LIST #9: FIGHTING WITH FAMILY ON CHRISTMAS

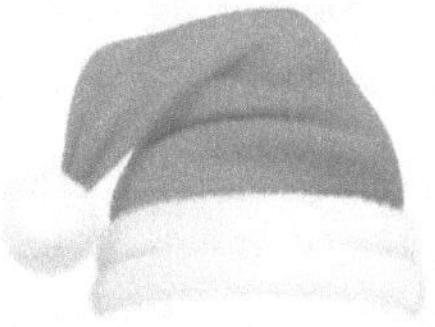

It was a little weird waking up on Christmas day knowing that I was going to spend it with Max and Danny. Danny had crawled into bed with us at some point in the night and I was warmly encased between their two hot bodies. I realized sadly that I was way more excited at the prospect of spending Christmas with these two men that I had just met than spending it with my Dad and the new life he had created for himself.

"What's with the resting Grinch face?" Danny asked, waggling his eyebrows playfully as I had learned he liked to do.

I snorted. 'It's Christmas," I responded, not answering his question.

Danny hopped out of bed. I was so busy devouring how delicious he looked in just a pair of low-hanging flannel Christmas pajamas that it took me a second to realize he was on the phone with room service ordering what appeared to be the whole menu.

"Guess he's hungry," came a gravelly voice in my ear as Max sat up behind me.

It hit me then that we had all been in bed together and I suddenly got shy. I practically ran from the room, yelling over my shoulder that I was going to get cleaned up.

I shut the door of my room and leaned against it, throwing my head back with a sigh. This was crazy. So crazy. They hadn't even seemed to mind that I had been with both of them. Maybe they did this regularly. Should I ask? No, I shouldn't ask. It's none of my business. Panicked thought after thought barreled through my mind. It didn't help that my phone was blowing up with text after text from my step-brother. I continued to ignore his attempts to contact me and concentrated on the problems I was facing at the moment.

I stayed in my room for at least fifteen minutes, pretending to get ready even though I didn't think we were leaving the suite. When I heard Danny answering the door for room service, I knew that I couldn't delay any longer.

I opened the door. Max sent me a questioning look, but I ignored it, pasting on a smile that quickly turned real when I saw how excited Danny was about the amount of food he had ordered.

I forgot all about my panic in the ensuing hours as we lost ourselves in what seemed like every breakfast food on the planet and Home Alone 1-3. We cuddled and kissed; the guys seemed to have no problem with affection in front of each other. Danny made both Max and I laugh with Christmas pun after Christmas pun. The snow fell softly outside, and the view was as Christmassy as you could get from the living room's floor to ceiling windows.

It was the most perfect Christmas I could remember since my mother had been alive.

I looked away from The Santa Claus that was playing on the big-screen when Danny suddenly fell on the couch beside me, tossing a red and gold wrapped present into my lap.

"What is this?" I asked in surprise.

"Just open it," Danny said with a cheeky smile.

"But..."

"Just open it," growled Max playfully from the other side of me.

With trembling hands, I carefully unwrapped the gift. Danny was vibrating with excitement next to me. I gasped when I saw that it was a first edition of The Christmas Carol by Charles Dickens.

"How did you...?" I gasped, putting one hand over my mouth in shock as tears threatened to fall. I had mentioned to them the first night that my mother had read it to me every Christmas and it was one of my favorite books and memories. I couldn't believe they had gotten it for me.

"This is too expensive. I can't accept it," I cried even as I lovingly stroked the cover.

"I saw it in that rare books store that was across the street from the ice bar before you guys met up with me, and I knew you had to have it," explained Max.

"I helped pay for it," interjected Danny loudly. I shot him an amused grin.

"Thank you. This is so perfect," I told them, holding the

book close to my chest. "Except I didn't get you guys anything," I moaned suddenly.

"That's quite alright," said Danny, pulling me into his lap. "I'm pretty sure that you've given me some unforgettable gifts over the last few days," he joked as he began to tickle me. I knew I had turned scarlet in color as I thought about our interlude in the mall and the red ribbon scene from yesterday. Max just gave me that trademark smirk of his when I made the mistake of looking at him. He knew exactly what I was thinking about.

They stopped teasing me finally and we settled in to finish our movie. When Danny decided to order some hot chocolate, I decided to run downstairs and grab a bottle of peppermint schnapps from the hotel shop downstairs. I had seen it the other day when we had been perusing what they had for snacks and I knew it would be a perfect way to end the day. "Tis the Season" and all of that...

I was walking through the lobby when an uneasy feeling crept up my spine. It felt like someone was watching me. I looked over my shoulder, but no one looked out of the ordinary. Shaking it off, I walked into the store and made my purchase.

Out in the hall, I gripped my plastic bag with the bottle and headed toward the elevator. It was Christmas, after all, and a special drink was a must. I fiddled with the bag when someone stepped out in front of me from an alcove branching out from the hall.

They stepped in my way as I tried to shuffle out of their way.

"Hello, Belle."

When I heard that voice, my entire body went rigid, the sound sickening me to my stomach, I lifted my gaze.

"Todd?" his name fell from my mouth like a stone

sinking to the bottom of the sea. My feet already slipped backward, taking me farther from him.

He groaned, like he always did when I pushed away from him. Spearing his hand through his short dark hair, he glared at me with those large brown eyes crowned by the thickest brows. His upper lip quirked at the edges.

"You don't seem happy to see me, *sis*."

"What are you doing here? Have you resorted to stalking me now?" My words trembled and I glanced up the empty hall with reception farther ahead. But no one was here to help me quickly get past him without him making a scene.

His eyes flickered behind him and back at me like he'd read my mind, then he lashed a hand out and grabbed me by the throat before hauling me into the shadowy alcove and slamming my back to the wall.

"You think it's funny to ignore my messages? I pour my heart out to you, and you think it's a big joke."

My heart was pounding so loud, my flesh covered in cold shivers, and I was surprised Todd couldn't hear it as he stood so close, studying every inch of me. It made me sick to my stomach.

Those dark eyes pierced into me as my breaths wheezed from my lungs. I was barely drawing breath while this monster was glaring at me.

Fury whipped through me, and I fiddled to grab hold of the bottle in the bag. When I finally gripped the neck, I swung it up and into the side of his head.

He released me and roared with pain as he clasped his head.

I stumbled on my feet; my knuckles white from holding the bottle so tight. "Are you a psycho? I'm not interested in you. You're my step brother and nothing more. I've made it clear for so long I want nothing to do with you." I hated him more than I thought possible, but on the inside, I was terrified of what else he was capable of. And my throat ached from where he had seized me.

His gaze locked on me as he tilted his head back, a sneer on his lips, and hatred spewed from his expression.

"The thing is, *princess*," he said, his voice mocking me. "I've already made the decision for you, and I always get what I want."

My head was spinning. Who was this lunatic?

When he stepped closer, I backed away, my hackles raised as was my bottle of Schnapps. "Come any closer, and I'll scream, and then you'll bleed a lot." I waved my weapon.

But he moved so fast, I barely had time to react. With a swing of his hand, he knocked the bottle from my hand, sending it flying and bouncing over the carpeted floor, barely making a sound. His other hand grabbed my wrist and he hauled me toward him with unimaginable strength, pivoting me to look away from him as he hooked his arm around my throat.

"Now, sis, you're coming with me to spend Christmas at a nice hotel I got us." His hand reached for my breast, squeezing, and I gagged with disgust.

Thrusting an elbow into his gut, he tightened his grip around my neck.

My voice came out as muffled sounds. Panic rocked through me that somehow, he'd take me, and no one would know where I ended up. I couldn't even bare to think of what waited for me in his hotel room.

One minute, Todd was choking me, the next he was gone, and I scrambled forward and snatched the bottle from the floor. I spun, my lungs filled, a scream pressing on the back of my throat. Except it wasn't him standing there, but Danny, concern creasing his brow. Max shoved Todd into the wall, snarling at him like a predator. My heart soared at seeing them. I rushed to Danny, and he embraced me, kissing my brow.

"Did he hurt you?" His fingers trailed over my neck, probably red from Todd's fingers.

I was shaking my head. "That's my step brother. He's creepy as hell and has been messaging me for days all kinds of shit. I didn't even know he was here until he snuck up on me."

Danny pushed me to stand behind him as he went to help Max.

My stepbrother was wiping the back of his hand across his bloodied mouth, fury behind those dark eyes that promised retribution.

"You little whore. Are they the reason you didn't return my messages?"

I was scared to hell and back, shaking uncontrollably.

Max turned to me. "Who is this asshole?"

"Her stepbrother," Danny answered. "He put bruises on her, he needs to be taught a lesson."

I couldn't find my words, but just stared as Danny and Max lunged for my stepbrother, each grabbing an arm and hauling him down the hall. I recoiled as he roared and fought against the guys, but he was nothing compared to them. They easily overpowered him.

All I could do was stand and stare in shock. No one had ever fought for me this way.

Danny shoved open the stairwell door and they pushed Todd through, both of them rushing in after him. The door shut with a loud clap behind them.

My stomach churned and hurt, and I chewed on a hangnail as I paced back and forth, not wanting them to get in trouble because of my dickhead stepbrother.

Mumbled voices sounded, and a loud thud that smacked into the door came from the stairwell. I stepped closer but waited. Todd needed to be taught a lesson and had to leave me alone. I reached up and ran my fingers over my sore neck where he'd grabbed me, where evidently bruises were already forming.

After what felt like a lifetime, the door swung open and Max emerged, then Danny, and behind him I caught a quick glimpse of my brother before the door shut. He sat on the step, his lip busted open, blood dripping from his cheek, his clothes ruffled. He stared at the ground; shoulders curled forward. But I didn't feel an ounce of guilt for him. Not when he didn't understand boundaries or what "no" meant.

"Let's go upstairs, gorgeous." Max wrapped an arm around my waist and drew me tight against him like he had no plans to ever let me out of his sight. He walked away.

I was shaken up at seeing Todd. He was a stalker, and I wanted him nowhere near me ever again.

The elevator door closed behind us, and I was gasping for air, my arms trembling as I clutched the bottle to my chest.

"He's not going to ever touch you." Danny approached me and took the Schnapps from my death grip. Then he collected me into his arms, and I pressed myself against his chest, inhaling his hypnotizing scent, feeling safer with these two men then I had my whole life. Max stood at my back, and the three of us didn't break apart until we reached our floor. They stayed close and something in my heart clenched at having these two strong protectors care for me that much.

"No one's ever done that for me before," I admitted.

"While we're around, no one will ever hurt you again,"

Max promised. And I took that promise and secured it in my heart.

Out in the hallway, I pushed myself on tippy toes and kissed Danny, which turned into something passionate and deep and intoxicating. I turned my head and Max greeted me with a kiss of his own, embracing my mouth with his.

Their hands were all over me, and I was suddenly swept into their world. Me kissing two men, having them with me at once.

"We should head back to the room if we're continuing this," I whispered, my words breathy.

The boys exchanged a glance, then rushed me toward the room. My heart was thumping in my chest at what I had implied, but I wanted this. I craved their affection.

NAUGHTY LIST #10: TWO AT ONCE

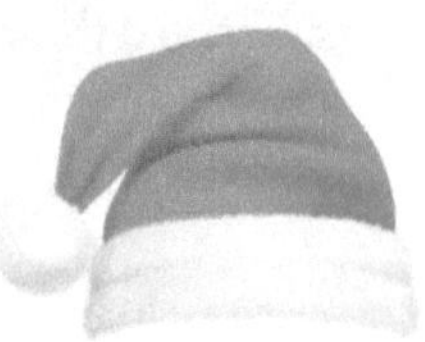

A few days ago, I assumed my life was fine. It was to a point. I was completely happy with the path I'd traveled and doing the right thing had always brought me happiness. I wasn't saying I lived a horrible life. Far from the truth, but what I had realized since meeting Max and Danny was that I'd played it too safe for too long. There were so many things I missed out on by not staying out late, studying endlessly on weekends, and telling myself I didn't have time for a boyfriend. Excuses?

Maybe. Or maybe it was just fear.

Now, I pushed aside all inhibition and stood there, blushing wildly, gape-mouthed that I had suddenly found two gorgeous men who were willing to protect me.

They stared at me like I might be a piece of chocolate

cake. Both sets of gazes slid over me, bringing butterflies to life in my stomach. Danny with his chiseled cheekbones, stunning blue eyes, and his knee-buckling winks. Max and his stoic expression, the devilish sneaky grin he always gave, and the rare sexy grins that flooded me with so much warmth when he gave them to me. I couldn't believe these two gods wanted me! At the same time!

My legs wobbled under me.

Never in my wildest dreams had I imagined I'd gain the attention of a hot guy, but two... I needed to fan myself.

Since meeting them they'd piled on the compliments, sweet words, grazing touches that drove me crazy. The sex with each was mind blowing. Now I was completely theirs.

Danny was unbuttoning his shirt, and I was shivering with anticipation. "You okay with this? You okay with being with us both?" he asked, his finger tracing down his bare chest, tanned and muscular and so damn hot.

My hands tingled with the need to reach out and touch him. How could I say no to such perfection?

Max simply watched me like he'd forgotten how to breathe.

My heart was racing. I'd never felt like this before, not this intense where the heat between my legs felt like liquid fire. I could barely keep my hormones in check, and maybe I didn't want to.

"Yes," the word flew from my lips, and I was trembling ridiculously with excitement. I was ready to become their dessert. Danny pushed the shirt down strong, thick arms, and my breath hitched all the way down to my lungs.

Max pulled his up and over his body, and my mouth dropped at the sight of his ripped stomach...those hard pecs. Who were these guys, built like they belonged on the runway? He took his pants and boxers off in one go, and then he was naked. My gaze was swinging from one to the other, not wanting to miss anything.

Their skin seemed to glow beneath the fireplace's flickering flames.

Both stood there with no shirts, just incredibly delicious bare chests, tapering at the waist in a perfect V, and I craved running my hands along every hard plane.

Danny wasn't waiting and I had to laugh as he popped open the buttons of his jeans and dropped them in two seconds, revealing he'd been going commando all day. His erection stood upright and so hard, I struggled to look anywhere else. He grasped his thick cock. "You think you can handle this, naughty girl?"

I would have laughed out loud at his corniness if I wasn't completely and utterly mesmerized.

"Come here, sexy." He reached out a hand and I placed my fingers in his. He drew me closer, my feet stumbling forward, my stomach in knots. This was new for me, and I was so freaking excited, I could barely contain myself. My gaze flipped from one guy to the next, and each time they touched me, my skin rippled with goosebumps, a zip of electricity racing through me. The sensation dipped to between my thighs, and I knew that with one touch I'd explode.

Two chests pressed against me, hands all over my body, exploring, teasing. Me sandwiched between two sexy-as-hell naked guys, and I was thrumming like never before.

Me.

The good girl everyone said I was.

Me.

The one who never stepped a foot wrong.

Me.

The girl who'd just found her new favorite thing in the world.

They pulled and tugged my clothes off me, and I stood there letting them. Encouraging it with a smile, adoring the way they looked at me with eyes sparkling, mouths parted, breaths racing. Danny who stood behind me, unclasped my bra and slowly slid the straps down my arms, his mouth following the path until my bra fell to my feet.

Max's strong hands unzipped my jeans and pushed them down together with my underwear. I stepped out of them, and he pushed all our clothes aside.

Danny's hands were on my hips, his touch so hot. Fingers slid high, skimming under my breasts.

I took in a sharp, shaky breath.

His hands rose to cover my breasts, fitting perfectly into each palm. He squeezed them, his lips on my shoulder covering me in tender kisses. A moan slipped past my throat and I was blushing insanely at standing naked with them. We stared at each other, but I wasn't backing away.

Max neared, his hands on my hips, mouth on mine, and he kissed me like the world was ending. Desperate and full of emotion. Pressing his tongue against the seam of my lips, I parted my mouth to accept him, tasting his muskiness, falling under his spell.

He dropped to his knees in front of me, and I shivered with anticipation, with nerves. I'd only been with one guy before and he was terrible, not understanding what the word foreplay meant.

Nothing compared to Danny and Max. Nothing.

Max left a line of kisses across my stomach, sliding lower and lower. I tensed as his attention dipped to between my thighs, his tongue flickering, finding my searing heat.

Danny held me up, his hands kneading my breasts, and I was already floating.

"You're sexy as sin," Max murmured. "I love the way you taste and smell." His hand slid to my ankle gingerly and lifted it from the floor, his fingers skimming to my knee and he placed it over his shoulder. He shifted closer, prying open my thighs for easier access.

Without ceremony, he pressed his mouth to me. I inhaled sharply, and he watched me. I felt like we were connected in that moment, all three of us.

His face was buried between my thighs, devouring me. Licking. Teasing, Tugging. He was relentless, sucking on my clit. I moaned with arousal, and a trickle of my wetness was running down the inside of my thighs as I began to move against his mouth seeking more.

Max never stopped, he pressed his tongue into me, then stroked me deeper.

It felt incredible. Max knew exactly where to lick, where to nibble. How to make me shake. I was short of breath while the muscles in my legs were trembling.

Danny devoured my neck, his fingers pinching my hardened nipples, and I was so close, the climax swelling, building through me.

The sounds Max made were intoxicating, his tongue devious, and I was melting beneath him and Danny.

They were drop-dead gorgeous, and I was being worshipped and ravished so intensely, I was lost to them. "Please never stop," I murmured.

Danny laughed so sexily in my ear, I trembled with a craving I'd never experienced before.

Max's teasing continued when he pushed two fingers inside me, stretching me. I stiffened at first, and he slid in and out of me, the tips of his fingers pressing right against my G-spot. My breaths rushed, and as he pumped into me, a burst of white light flashed in my mind as I floated on their pleasure.

When Max released me from his grip, I groaned in protest, but he was on his feet, smiling so evilly, so beautifully that I reached out and brought him to me.

Mouth to mouth, our tongues tangled, and I tasted myself on him. Tasted him, and I loved it more than I thought I would.

Max broke away, and Danny wrapped me up in his arms before lifting me off my feet and laying me down on the white fur rug in front of the fireplace.

The heat was so inviting, so comforting. I stared up at my men, who looked down at me, admiring. Their starved gazes filled me with a bravado I hadn't felt before.

I ran a hand over my breast and plucked at my hardened nipple, tugging it.

Max reached down and gripped his cock, his eyes glazed over.

I swallowed hard, loving to see them succumb to their desires, to see what I did to them.

Danny fell to his knees in front of me with intense devotion in those spectacular blue eyes. His fingers touched the tips of my curled toes and traced them up my legs to my knees. He pried them open, his gaze falling between my thighs, and his grin told me everything. He adored everything he saw.

He reached over to his wallet in his pants and pulled out a condom. He had himself covered in seconds, then he pressed himself between my legs, his body over me. His body ablaze against mine, and I reached out to his neck and the side of his face, stretching my neck up to meet his mouth. I kissed him like he was the man of my dreams and I couldn't imagine myself being anywhere else.

The tip of his cock kissed my entrance, and I raised my hips to better meet him. His lips were on my neck, his breath covering me in shivers, and whispers driving me insane. "I'm going to fuck you now."

"Please, stop teasing," I said in the softest of voices, hands gripping his shoulders, nails digging into flesh.

He leaned closer and kissed me as he buried himself in me. I moaned loudly against his mouth, feeling him stretching me, filling me completely. He took me fast, thrusting into me, back and forth, pinning me beneath him.

I heaved for each breath, my body shuddering beneath him.

In one swift move, he tucked his arms behind my back, and lifted us to his knees, him still hilt deep inside me, his muscles strained, but he didn't hesitate. The strength to hold me like this was astonishing.

"You're mine, and so beautiful," he growled. Shuffling, he stretched out his legs underneath me, so he was sitting, but true to his word, he never released me. "Now show me how you ride me."

He lay back on the rug, and I straddled him, moving my hips up and down on his shaft, loving how he rubbed my insides, how the friction ignited a blaze of its own.

That was when I felt Max at my back, his hand stroking the length of my spine, fingers falling deeper over my ass, falling to where I grew so wet. He swept his fingers back up, and gently rubbed my rear entry. "You're so wet."

I flinched, never having been touched there before.

"Are you okay with this?" he asked in my ear.

I was floating on so much arousal, needing these men

like no other, and the more his thumb rubbed me in that spot, the closer I moved to the edge of my orgasm.

"Please be gentle with me," I said.

"Oh baby, I would never be anything else with someone as gorgeous and delicate as you."

"Delicate?" I glanced over my shoulder at him with a raised brow and laughed, remembering our time in the bedroom and me tied up.

"Yes," he answered as his finger slid into me.

"Ohh." My muscles tightened at first, and Danny beneath me moaned.

Danny smirked up at me. "I love how you squeeze my cock that way."

"Open up for me, babe," Max commanded.

I turned my gaze to him once again and followed his request, taking a deep inhale and releasing it. I didn't know why except that I wanted this, needed to have them tonight. I let my legs fall wider and I leaned over Danny, who took a nipple into his mouth and sucked it between his teeth. "You have perfect tits," he groaned.

Max's fingers worked into me and I never knew arousal could feel this incredibly good. He removed his finger and I heard the crinkly sound of a condom, then he sidled up behind me, his erection sliding along the silkiness of my backside. He guided his tip to my entrance, while Danny remained inside me, all of us unmoving.

"Oh, Fudge," I whimpered as Max slowly pushed into me, taking his time.

"Just relax babe and let me in." His voice was raw and full of sexual hunger.

I'd never felt so wicked, so devious, and I loved every second of it. So I calmed my breaths, and Max pushed himself deeper into me.

With both of them fully inside me, I was panting, loving how it felt to take two guys at once, and in slow motion Max pulled and pushed into me, in and out, and I fell into a rhythm with him, riding Danny at the same time, who was groaning. The three of us were this perfect unit, connected, working through our pleasures, gasping for air, and me, between them.

"Holy crap, if I don't belong on the naughty list now, nothing will get me there." I burst out laughing, which quickly morphed into moans of desire. And as if something unlocked inside me, I rocked with the orgasm that shoved through me so ferociously, I screamed out the relentless energy crashing through me. The pleasure shuddered; my muscles clenched from the dynamic burn owning me. I never wanted this sensation to end.

Both the guys moaned out at the same time as I squeezed them, they pulsed inside me, shuddering against me, riding the rollercoaster of orgasms with me.

When I couldn't take it any longer, I collapsed on top of Danny and he wrapped his arms around me, all of us sweaty and breathing hard. Max pulled out and got to his feet.

"I'm going to get a towel and clean you up gorgeous. Danny, bring her to bed."

I couldn't stop smiling and just laid in Danny's embrace convinced I'd somehow become the luckiest girl in the world. Not to mention, I'd just had sex with two of the hottest guys in the universe at the same time. Myles was going to die when she found out.

As I LAID between the two guys, listening to their soft breaths as they slept peacefully, I knew that I needed to get out of here. There was no way this wasn't going to end messy, not after what had just happened. I wasn't the girl who could do all of that and not feel something.

All we had promised was for a short break from reality, and they had given me that. For me to expect more from them wasn't fair. I was sure that they had feelings for me too, but the fact that we were at different schools meant we would never see each other. It would just never work.

We had all received an alert on our phones that flights were resuming now that the storm had worked its way through Chicago and then New York. There had been discussion about going to the airport together, but I knew as I slipped out of bed at three am, that I should just leave now.

I packed my stuff including the priceless book they had gotten me, and with one last look at them still sleeping, I left the hotel and headed for the airport.

There had been a flight with seats leaving an hour after I arrived at the airport. The stress of going through security and getting on the flight kept me occupied enough that the tears didn't start until the plane had started to take off.

I didn't stop crying until I landed in New York.

NAUGHTY LIST #11: FALL IN LOVE WITH STRANGERS

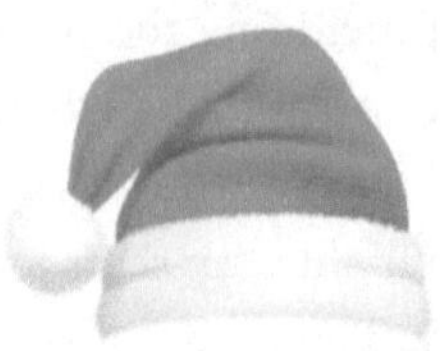

*B*eing at home was miserable. All I could think about was Danny and Max. But it was better this way. Our time together had been what we had agreed upon—a small blip in time. And I would always have it as my favorite memory. It almost seemed like a dream as I sat in my small bedroom in the Brooklyn brownstone that I'd grown up in.

I cringed when I heard my stepmother's screechy voice as she laid into my dad about something. She had been worse than usual since I arrived home, blaming me for ruining Christmas. She somehow blamed me for the storm, and the fact that her son wasn't coming home, even though I was pretty sure that he hadn't told them what had happened and so she had no idea he had even seen me. She had also laid into me for the fact that my father had apparently been upset that I hadn't made it home for Christmas and he had tried to get her to wait to open up her presents. As if a middle-aged woman should be upset about not opening her presents on time.

I sighed as I stared at the falling snow outside my window. Not for the first time, I wished that I had at least exchanged phone numbers with the guys. I could use a joke from Danny or Max's steadying presence right now.

I finally decided I needed to drag myself out of bed and go eat some breakfast. I went downstairs into the kitchen, preparing myself for more crap from 'mommy dearest'.

"Belle, you're awake," my dad said, and he almost sounded happy about it. I gave him a small smile and good morning and walked to the pantry to get breakfast.

"Are you really going to eat that?" Gloria snarked as I began to pour myself a bowl of cereal. "You know your body doesn't do well with carbs."

I rolled my eyes but said nothing, and of course neither did my father. I would have loved it if he actually stuck up for me once in a while. I didn't know why I still expected that since the last few years had consisted of him letting Gloria steamroll him at every moment.

"You got a letter from USC," my dad commented softly, laying an envelope next to my bowl. I put my spoon down and picked up the letter, ripping it open. It was information for graduation, the standard ordering forms for getting my cap and gown as well as information for parents on where to stay and when events took place.

"Do you need me to get a hotel reservation for you for graduation?" I asked my dad, sliding the packet over to him so he could look through it. Gloria grabbed it before he could pick it up.

"This is right in the middle of the trip we planned with Emily and Dave," Gloria complained to my father as she glanced through the packet. She looked up at me, a triumphant spark in her eyes. "Oh honey," she said in a fake voice. "We're not going to be able to make it. The tickets were non-refundable," she continued.

Horror-struck, I looked over at my father. "Please tell me that you aren't going on vacation instead of my college graduation," I begged him. But the look on his face said all I needed to know.

It was as if a match had been struck, and all of the anger and sadness that I been bottling up since my dad had married this awful woman came barreling out.

"You have got to be fucking kidding me," I yelled at him.

Gloria gasped, pretended to be upset over my reaction, even though I was pretty sure it was the first "f" word that I'd ever uttered in my life.

"For years, I've let you push me aside," I said coldly to my father.

He looked upset, but he still wasn't saying anything.

"I told myself that you deserve the chance to be happy since we lost Mom. That marrying *her* was what Mom would have wanted. But there's no way that she would've ever done this if the situation was reversed. You've made me feel like a burden for years, pushed aside anything that I needed. NEVER stood up for me." I took a deep breath before continuing. "Did you know that her disgusting son has been hitting on me for years?" I said, pointing to Gloria. "I've had to lock my door every time we were both home at the same time so that he didn't sneak into my bedroom in the middle of the night. These bruises are from him," I said, pointing to my neck.

My dad looked sick as Gloria began to furiously protest what a liar I was.

I looked at her. "Shut up," I told her, effectively silencing her with the vehemence in my voice. I pushed away from the counter and began to back out of the room. "You know what, you both deserve each other. I'm done." Looking straight at my father to make sure the message went through, I continued. "I don't care if I ever see you again," I said before leaving the room.

Once in my bedroom, I threw all my things into a bag, half expecting my dad to come up the stairs to try to make things right. When I was finished packing and he hadn't appeared, and I could hear Gloria screaming from downstairs, I knew he really wasn't coming.

I left the house that I'd grown up in without a backwards glance. It was expensive to move my flight, but I happily put it on my dad's credit card, a card I wouldn't be using after this. Paying for my flight back to school was the least he could do after everything he had put me through.

As the plane took off and I watched as New York disappeared from sight, I felt free for the first time in forever. My departure from reality with the guys had given me the courage to do something that I should have done a long time ago. Whatever happened in the future, I was going to channel the bravery of the Belle who had taken a chance on a wintry layover in Chicago.

THERE WAS a knock on my dorm door, and I frowned as I looked at the door as if it had offended me. I was in the middle of a really good book and I didn't want to take a break. I had no idea who was even in the dorm to bother me right now. I still had one more week of winter break before students needed to return for class and the campus was a ghost town except for the people on sports teams that had to come back early to practice. When another knock came, I sighed and set the book down. Whoever it was wasn't going to go away.

I was dressed in a pair of sweats and a ratty t-shirt and I looked like crap. It had been three days since I'd gotten back to school and there had been no word from my dad. I knew it was going to take a bit for it not to hurt even though I was proud of standing up for myself, but between that and leaving the guys...I wasn't in a good place.

I was swept into a pair of strong, familiar arms before I had even seen who was at the door.

"You are in so much fucking trouble," a voice growled.

Belatedly I realized that I was somehow in Max's arms. I allowed myself to sink into his embrace before asking any questions, closing my eyes as I squeezed him tight.

There was a gentle stroke on my face. When I opened my eyes, I saw Danny. Was this a dream?

Max let me go and Danny scooped me into his arms, squeezing me so tight that I let out a little grunt because I couldn't breathe.

"Whoops," said Danny, loosening his hold.

"What are you...?" I began to ask.

"If you hadn't snuck out of bed in the middle of the night we could have talked," chided Max.

"What were you thinking?" barked Danny very uncharacteristically.

I didn't really have an excuse to give them. It had been the fear of the unknown, the fear of rejection that had made me leave.

"I just didn't want you to feel pressure to make this more than it was," I told them lamely.

"More than it was?" repeated Max sarcastically. "You're so full of it, Belle. I thought you were past being scared of everything."

I didn't have a response to that. "What are you doing here?" I finally said.

"We're students here," replied Danny proudly.

"What? How?" I asked, my mouth hanging open.

"We petitioned to transfer at the beginning of last semester after our baseball coach got suspended because he got caught with a co-ed. The new coach they put in didn't have the major league contacts that we needed...and basically sucked balls. Max here is one of the top prospects in the country, and I'm not half bad myself, so we got the okay to transfer at the end of the semester," explained Danny.

I took a moment to absorb all of that. Baseball. That made sense based on their unbelievable bodies. And the fact that they were here early since I knew the baseball team was one of the teams that had to report back to get ready for their season.

"So, you're going to be students here?" I asked once again just to clarify.

"Yep," said Danny, pulling me against him and wrapping his arms around me tightly. I soaked in the affection after days of loneliness.

"Why didn't you tell me?" I asked, frowning because I had told them where I went to school.

Max looked sheepish for a moment. "We've had a lot of girls try to get with us once they knew we were pretty big baseball players. I'm set to go first or second round in the draft and I just wanted to hang out with you without having to wonder if you were just around because you wanted something from me."

I nodded thoughtfully. That made sense. Hadn't I wanted to be someone different during that time as well?

"We were going to tell you everything, make plans, do this thing right that morning," said Danny.

Max crowded me against Danny so that I was buffeted by both of their bodies. "Are you done running, pretty girl?" said Max as he reached out a hand to stroke my bottom lip.

"You want to be with me?" I asked somewhat incredulously. "Both of you? Because I really can't decide between the two of you," I told him.

They both got even closer to me until I felt like I was going to faint from the hormones that were building up inside of me with their close proximity.

"We both like you, a lot. Actually...I'm pretty sure we both have fallen in love with you," Danny whispered in a sexy voice as my heart began to beat out of my chest. "We want to see where this goes. Will you give us a chance, Belle?"

"Will you, sweetheart?" asked Max, staring at me with those intense eyes of his. "Take a chance on two assholes you met in an airport bar?"

I thought for a moment, looking between the two of them. I remembered how captivated I was the first time we met, how they shared their table with me, ate my nachos, then bought me drinks. I'd never forget the days I spent with them in Chicago. And it hit me that I had fallen in love with them somewhere along the way despite my best intentions. They were giving me what I had thought was only a dream.

"Yes," I whispered, giving them a soft smile as I began to softly sob.

Max responded with only a smile before his lips were on

mine, kissing me with days of pent-up passion. Danny started trailing kisses down my neck at the same time and it was like we had never been a part.

The room was filled with the rustling of clothing and soft moans as we got reacquainted with each other, and I had never been happier.

I may have gotten myself on the naughty list, but I had somehow gotten everything I could have ever wanted for Christmas and so much more.

EPILOGUE

(MAXWELL)

Graduation day was here, and I was so fucking proud of our girl. Danny and I were both on our feet hooting and hollering as she crossed the stage in her black graduation robe and cap.

She shot us a shy glance right before she accepted her diploma. Our girl was gorgeous. Yes, that's right. I said, "our girl." It had become obvious quite quickly after we met, that we both could see a future with her. Danny and I had spent this past spring semester playing baseball and figuring out our relationship with Belle. It hadn't always been easy, and sometimes one or both of us had gotten jealous. But it had been so worth it.

I looked over at Danny who was practically vibrating with excitement and pride as he watched her. Our names had been called earlier and Danny had already taken off his cap and rolled the sleeves of his graduation gown up, showcasing those tattoos he was so proud of. I have never imagined sharing the love of my life, but if I had to do it, I couldn't picture doing it with a better guy.

I had always thought that Danny and I were going to go pro together, but halfway through baseball season when we were both getting looks from major league scouts, Danny had told me that his heart just wasn't in it. Baseball was still my dream however, and they were both so fucking supportive about it despite the fact that me being drafted meant that they would be trying to find jobs in Atlanta, since I would be starting with the AA team there.

I knew the next few years would be hard as I hopefully battled my way up to a spot with the Braves, but I knew with Belle and Danny beside me, I could make it through anything. I knew it would make it easier to be on the road for away games knowing that Belle was being taken care of by someone who loved her just as much as I did.

I looked for Belle again and smiled when I saw that she was standing by her dad taking a bouquet of flowers from him. Yes, he was here. Evidently the thought of losing Belle had been enough to bring him to his senses. He was in the middle of a nasty divorce from Belle's stepmother, but he seemed lighter somehow, and he would tell anyone who would listen that he was happier than ever. And we believed him.

It was still going to take a while for him to rebuild his relationship with his daughter, but they had made a lot of great strides over the past few months. And the fact that he had a lot of groveling to do with her had helped him more easily accept the fact that his daughter was dating two guys at once.

Danny was already out of his seat and heading towards Belle even though the ceremony wasn't over yet, and I gave up with propriety and followed him to our girl.

Danny picked her up and swung her around, making a huge scene as he laid a loud smacking kiss on her lips. Belle pretended that he was embarrassing her, but the flush in her cheeks and the shine in her eyes let me know that she loved it.

I grabbed Belle from Danny when I was tired of waiting and gave her a deep kiss that had us both breathless when it ended. I knew there were a ton of shocked and curious people watching us, but the semester had been good in getting us used to that. When people realized that there wasn't anything dramatic going on, just two guys in love with the same girl who happened to be best friends, they moved on and it had stopped being a big deal.

We took the obligatory pictures after the ceremony officially ended, and then started to walk out to the parking lot to get a celebratory dinner. Danny had Belle on his back-piggyback style, and I laughed as he almost dropped her. Belle's dad was watching them with a small little smile on his face. I knew that he was happy to see Belle happy, even though he didn't totally agree with it.

Belle turned her head to look for me and a smile lit up her face when we locked eyes. I was never going to get tired of that fucking beautiful smile. I especially liked it when she gave it to me in the bedroom, a place we would be going to sooner rather than later today, I hoped.

I patted the ring box that I had taken to carrying with me everywhere I went. Danny and I were going to propose to her, we were just waiting to find the perfect moment. I wasn't sure how much longer I was going to be able to wait. It was going to happen soon.

I didn't know how I'd gotten so lucky this last Christmas to get such a perfect gift, one that I hadn't even known I'd wanted. But I was never going to take Belle for granted. Belle was my happily ever after, and I would always have Santa to thank for that.

The End

SNEAK PEAK

Have you discovered School of Broken Souls yet? Here's a sneak peek at the first chapter...

SCHOOL OF BROKEN SOULS

Adeline Jones is perfectly average. Or at least she thinks she is until she receives an invite to attend Raven Academy, complete with a full scholarship. Raven Academy is the mysterious school that only the elite of the elite go and despite Adeline's misgivings about giving up her whole life to attend, there's no way her parents are going to let her give up such an opportunity.

But things at Raven Academy aren't what they seem. Everyone is a little too perfect, a little too rich, and a little too powerful for any normal student population. Things only complicate further when Adeline catches the eyes of Raven Academy's group of elite boys.

Can Adeline figure out what secrets Raven Academy is hiding before it's too late? Or will the price of admission to the elite academy be more than she can pay...like perhaps her soul.

EPIGRAPH

Deep into that darkness peering, long I stood there, wondering, fearing, doubting, dreaming dreams no mortal ever dared to dream before.
  -Edgar Allen Poe

1

———

I grip the gun under my coat, and my hand shakes. All of me trembles.

What the hell am I doing here?

A drop of sweat slides down my back. It must be a hundred degrees in this store. Or maybe my nerves are just making me feel like I'm in the living embodiment of hell.

A sudden shriek has me jumping in my boots, and I flinch around to see a child stomping his feet when his mom takes away a bag of fruit snacks that's he's poached from one of the shelves. *Listen to your mother*, I want to say, but I can't find my voice. Not now.

Not when I'm ready to run and hide.

But I have to see this through. People are counting on me. And I can't let them down.

I won't let them down.

I glance around at who else is in the store. There's a teenage couple making eyes at each other in the row over, and a grizzly old man looking over the beer aisle, but other than that the store's empty. I need everyone to leave before I do this though. This stupid, crazy, impossible thing.

I go through my plan again in my mind for the hundredth time. The gun is filled with water... a toy gun. But it will do the trick. *Please God let it work.*

The first time my friend Cody pointed it at me, I screamed. It sure as hell looks like a real handgun. The toy mirrors a Glock G43. I have no idea what the number means, but it's black and looks real. That's what matters.

Hopefully, the store clerk will think the same. And then when inevitably the police pick me up, maybe they will take it easier on me since it isn't a real gun. At least that's my hope, but I know I'm just fooling myself. I have to lie to myself, or I'll never go through with this.

I need the money.

I need it despite the fact that I've always been a good girl, the type of girl who never walks outside the lines or does anything unexpected.

Until now.

Robbing a 7-11 is definitely going to yank that title from me fast. And if that is the worse it does, I'll take it.

Sweat is rolling down my back now. It slides under the waistband of my jeans and beneath the elastic of my underwear. Why is it so hot in here?

I think again of the other night when I walked into the kitchen at midnight and found mom crying over a stack of bills. Dad withers away in their dark bedroom, too weak to come out, and too proud to ask for help from anyone.

There's a surgery that can help him, a surgery that can fix my family. But we need money for it.

I hated the word.

Need.

Just as much as I loathe the cancer slowly taking my dad from me.

My throat chokes, and I struggle to breathe. I glance around, finding the sliding door as the young couple leave.

Escape.

It's there for me. But it won't help my family.

I work two jobs after school and save every penny. But $8.00 an hour doesn't add up fast. I often talk to mom about maybe dropping out of school for a little bit, but she won't listen to me and threatens to make me quit my other jobs if I even mention it again. My mother and I both work as much as possible, but it's never going to be enough. Or at least it's never going to be enough in time to actually save my dad.

Another review of the store reveals three people wandering around the aisles, and this will be the best I can hope for. I swallow past a dry throat, my finger twitching on the gun handle, and I meander toward the only working cash register. The guard is at lunch, and I see no cameras. This is the right time, but hesitation slows me.

Dad. I have to think of him. Losing him isn't an option, and the doctors say with the right amount of money, he stands a damn good chance to heal.

I want that chance, so with squared shoulders, I march closer to the young girl picking at her nails behind the register. She's wearing her blue hair in a high ponytail and she has a small piercing in her nose.

My thoughts tangle into a web while fear squeezes my chest. What if I get caught? Mom and Dad will be horrified.

Shaking my head, I push that thought out of my mind. I can't let those thoughts creep in, or they'll cripple me. It took me three weeks to work up the courage to finally take action.

So, I have to do this.

I need this.

Fuck.

I lick my dry lips and approach the young girl. She looks up at me, disinterested, and my attention falls to her name tag.

Mary Sue.

I almost laugh out loud at the simpleness of her name, the cliché of it, but she distracts me.

"What do you have?" She eyes me up and down, seeing no groceries in my hand.

My mouth opens, but nothing comes out, and I will my hand to move. To pull out that damn gun. Sweat rolls down my neck.

"If you're gonna order cigarettes, I need to see an ID." She folds her arms across her chest.

My free hand juts out and I grab a handful of gum from a rack of candy, then dump them on the counter. Six packets. She starts scanning them, and I inch the gun out from under my coat, the words of what I'll say roll through my mind.

Stick'em up.

Stupid. So stupid. She won't take me seriously. What am I thinking?

I hold the gun low between me and the counter. I'm inches from showing her the weapon. *I can do this*; I keep repeating in my mind.

"Want a bag with these?" she barks, and I flinch so hard, I hit the gun's trigger and it squirts water across the bottom section of the counter near my feet. A light hiss sounds.

Shit!

"Yes, yes," I say, hoping she didn't hear the noise.

She cocks an eyebrow. "Really? You want a whole bag for six packets of gum. What about saving the environment?"

I flick my gaze up. "Then why did you ask? And yes, I want the bag."

She rolls her eyes and sighs as she leans over to grab one.

I lift the gun, placing it just over the counter, pointing it at Mary Sue, my body concealing the weapon should anyone behind me come to the register.

I can barely breathe when the front doorbell chimes. From the corner of my eye, I spot the navy uniform, the hulking form of the guard.

Fuck. Fuck. Fuck.

I shove the gun back into my coat and retreat from the counter, lowering my head.

"Hey, ma'am," Mary Sue calls out. "You forgot your six gums in a bag?" she says sarcastically.

The guard stands in my way in front of the glass door, and I freeze, about to fall apart. When I glance up, he studies me.

"You okay, Miss?"

"Y...yeah, of course." My voice trembles, and I sidestep him, sliding through the door. The bell gives another ring as I pass, startling me. The cool air does nothing to cool me down, not when my heart pounds inside me, and my mind screams the word *run* in my head.

A quick look behind me shows that the guard and girl are staring at me through the window. I'm sure they think I stole something. I turn away and walk fast down the sidewalk. The moment I take the corner, I run, still holding the gun under my coat. Over my shoulder, no one follows. I did nothing wrong, but still, I can't stop sprinting past people meandering on the sidewalk. A man in a suit bumps into me, but I keep going without apology.

I berate myself as I run for chickening out, for failing. I

won't be able to return to that 7-11 again, they'll remember me next time for sure because of my odd behavior.

I made a mess of everything today. I'll have to start again, find another location with no guard. I can't stop, not until I find a way to get money for Dad's surgery.

Finally, I slip into a quiet alley and press my back to a brick wall, gasping for air.

"Idiot," I mumble under my breath. If I moved faster, I'd now have a bag of cash. I rack my brain for the best store to steal from. Maybe I should have come up with a backup plan before this like in the movies. On those shows, they make it seem so easy, their plans go off without a hitch. In real life, I just suck and fail at everything.

I contemplate the locations I can try next, which ones would be potential hot spots. The bakery is quiet after the morning rush, except the owner stays in the back, so he might easily see me. The bookstore is always empty, there are rumors that it's going out of business which means they won't have a lot of cash on hand. I need one big hit, not small ones.

Then I remember the new pawn store. I shove the gun into the big pocket of my coat and take a deep inhale before stepping out of the alley.

Several blocks later, I stand outside the pawn store, studying the window filled with men's wristwatches and used cell phones.

Someone walks into me, hitting me so hard that I fall against the window, and spin around. "Hey!"

"Watch out," a young kid snipes at me as he rushes by.

"I was standing still," I call out, annoyed.

I really must be invisible as this type of thing happens more often than not.

I head inside the store. The walls are full of merchandise, and it smells like worn socks. An L-shaped glass counter sits against the back wall, and there are three assistants present, but no registers. I observe a customer paying for her merchandise by handing over money to a sales clerk who heads out past a shut door. He uses a card around his neck to open the door. This is a lot more complicated than the register at the convenience store.

A sales guy strolls toward me with a smile. I turn and head outside, putting quick distance between me and the store. That place is not going to work, so I keep walking, not ready to return home and face my parents. Not that they'll know what I'm doing but the hurt in their eyes, the hope to keep fighting will eat me up because I failed my mission.

It's not long before I find myself in front of Nico's Cafe, the local chain coffee shop, and the aroma of coffee draws me inside. I pluck out a freebie card from my wallet in my back pocket. They handed these out a few weeks ago.

I order myself a skim latte with vanilla syrup. With it in hand, I slide into a small booth and enjoy the small luxury of a hot brew in my hands and the tranquil sound of a soft song overhead.

A loud, sharp laugh shatters the peace, and I turn towards the sound.

I spot them and cringe. Two girls in miniskirts followed by three guys mock punching each other, strolling in my direction.

My stomach drops, and I slide in my seat, keeping my head low. Last time I bumped into Alexia, the blonde with legs for miles, she shoved me aside muttering about someone daring to be in her way.

I don't need snobby shitheads like them making this day even worse.

Their laughter makes me groan on the inside.

"Alexia is such a bae. I love her," Talia, the other girl says, and they both giggle, while I sip my coffee, wondering how I can slip past them without being seen. I'm so low in the social hierarchy at school, you would think they wouldn't even notice me. Too bad that hasn't stopped them from being assholes towards me when they get the chance.

Swallowing my last mouthful of sweet coffee, I grow tired of listening to their drivel.

"Did you see what that bitch, Olivia posted about you online?" Alexa asks, venom lining her voice. "We'll make her regret it tomorrow."

Talia snorts and the guys laugh in response. "She's pissed because she didn't get accepted into Raven Academy. They rejected her fat ass." Talia breaks out in an unattractive, high pitched laugh, her friends joining her like baying hyenas, laughing at someone else's misery.

Raven Academy.

That sounds like something familiar... maybe it's a school for Edgar Allan Poe lovers? Or it could be a morgue. I type it into the search bar on my phone but find nothing. Was it a new term kind of like the "mile high club"?

"Heard the place's a hole," one of the guys says. "The school is run down and only weirdos go there. My Dad knows someone that sent his kid there."

"I heard it's a cult," Alexia replies. "Pretty sure they pray to Satan or something else creepy like that."

"No, they don't," Talia giggles. "Or it would be in the news for sure."

"Unless they control the media," she whispers, in a menacing voice. "Haven't you seen those conspiracy shows I told you to watch about those organizations like the Illuminati? All kinds of shit is real."

I roll my eyes but remain glued to their conversation. I

ought to make my way out of the cafe, but I can't. Something about the name "Raven Academy" intrigues me. Not much happens in our town, well unless you count Mr. Chamberlain's death. He drank straight vinegar instead of apple cider vinegar for a new diet craze, and it burned his insides.

"Bet it's just a snooty Academy for the rich. And Olivia wasn't rich enough," another guy adds.

That definitely sounds more realistic, and I suspect that's why I haven't heard of the school. Out of my league.

My phone pings with a message.

Your dad isn't doing too well. You coming home soon? LOL

I type a response hastily to Mom.

Do you know what LOL means?

Two seconds later, her message flashes on my screen.

Love you lots.

I sigh and start typing when a shadow falls over me.

"Ghost girl." Alexia snaps. "Stop eavesdropping. Don't you have some other corner to lurk in?"

I jerk my head up, gritting my teeth, meeting her wry smirk. She glares down at me over the booth wall between us.

Breathing through my nostrils loudly, I grip my phone, refusing to engage, to give them fuel, to do anything with them.

Talia's head pops up alongside Alexia, her tight short curls bouncing around her head, making her look like a doll with a head too big for her body.

"What are you typing?" she asks.

"Shopping list," I lie and lower my head, unwilling to meet their eyes. Maybe they'll leave me alone. I tuck my phone into my pocket, already shuffling out of the booth in the opposite direction.

Alexia climbs to her feet and rounds my booth, standing there with her hands on her hips, staring at me. She hates me. Detests me. It's on her face. And I know why... three months ago one of her exes was stupid enough to ask me to the school dance. I put it down to him mocking me, and I turned him down. But that gave her enough ammunition to make me her enemy for life.

"He never liked you," she snarls, her upper lip curling. Her words are wicked and vicious.

"Told you before. He's not my type."

I stand from the booth and start toward the exit, ready to escape. It's what I'm good at, running, just like my failed robbery at the 7-11. The thought sinks through me, dampening my spirits even more. I brush my hands down my coat.

"What the hell are you wearing?" she curses at me, eyeing me up and down, scrunching her perfectly sculpted eyebrows as if my outfit offends her.

I lower my gaze and take a wide berth around her, but she snatches my arm, squeezing, her bony fingers feel like an iron grip.

"No one would ever be interested in a loser like you." Her fingernails press into the fabric, into my flesh, but I don't show the pain. I bite my lip so I can't make a sound.

I've mastered masking agony from when I keep Mom company as she cries, when I sit by Dad's bed when he's too tired to speak, when Alexia and the other girls attack me for no reason other than I exist. But after my day today, a fiery rage surges through me, and I find my voice.

Meeting her gaze, I spit the words and wrench my arm free, "Haven't you grown tired of this game yet? It's starting to bore me."

"Oh, so ghost girl has a backbone," Talia laughs the words, drawing attention from a few bystanders in the café.

Alexia takes another step closer, her face reddening.

I stand my ground, no matter how much my mind screams to turn and run. To leave because nothing good can come of this. My time is better spent elsewhere, and Mom is waiting for me. Dad isn't well.

Everyone's silent. I turn away when she grabs my hair and yanks me backward. Ow! I wince and reach for my head while others in the store gasp.

Someone is marching toward us.

Alexia is in my ear. "Do you think someone like you can threaten me?" She shoves her hand into my shoulder, and I stumble, rubbing the soreness spreading across my scalp, my heart racing. I'm pretty sure she pulled out a chunk of my hair.

The store manager is there all of a sudden, shoulders squared, towering over us. "Take it outside before I call the police."

I glare at Alexia, my cheeks on fire, tears in my eyes, and I fist my hands.

Nico, the owner appears next, stepping in front of me. "Go home, Adeline." He knows me, knows my parents, knows we're struggling. And I hate that because I don't want pity now or ever.

"I'll see you at school," Alexia snarls before whirling around and rejoining her friends.

So many eyes are on me, and I feel the weight of their

stares pinning me down. Their stares mix with the feeling of failure, the feeling of dread that is always with me.

I turn around and run out of the store. Only the sound of laughter follows me.

Read on at books2read.com/schoolofbrokensouls

ABOUT MILA YOUNG

Best-selling author, Mila Young tackles everything with the zeal and bravado of the fairytale heroes she grew up reading about. She slays monsters, real and imaginary, like there's no tomorrow. By day she rocks a keyboard as a marketing extraordinaire. At night she battles with her mighty pen-sword, creating fairytale retellings, and sexy ever after tales.

Ready to read more and more from Mila Young? www.subscribepage.com/milayoung

www.milayoungbooks.com

For more information...
mila@milayoungbooks.com

ABOUT C.R. JANE

A Texas girl living in Utah now, I'm a wife, mother, lawyer, and now author. My stories have been floating around in my head for years, and it has been a relief to finally get them down on paper. I'm a huge Dallas Cowboys fan and I primarily listen to Taylor Swift and hip hop...don't lie and say you don't too.

My love of reading started probably when I was three and it only made sense that I would start to create my own worlds since I was always getting lost in others'.

I like heroines who have to grow in order to become badasses, happy endings, and swoon-worthy, devoted, (and hot) male characters. If this sounds like you, I'm pretty sure we'll be friends.

I'm so glad to have you on my team...check out the links below for ways to hang out with me and more of my books you can read!

Visit my **Facebook** page to get updates.

Visit my Website.

Sign up for my newsletter to stay updated on new

releases, find out random facts about me, and get access to different points of view from my characters.

BOOKS BY C.R. JANE

www.crjanebooks.com

The Sounds of Us Contemporary Series (complete series)

Remember Us This Way

Remember You This Way

Remember Me This Way

Broken Hearts Academy Series: A Bully Romance (complete duet)

Heartbreak Prince

Heartbreak Lover

Ruining Dahlia (Contemporary Mafia Standalone)

Ruining Dahlia

Pretty Madness (Omegaverse Standalone)

Pretty Madness

The Fated Wings Series (Paranormal series)

First Impressions

Forgotten Specters

The Fallen One (a Fated Wings Novella)

Forbidden Queens

Frightful Beginnings (a Fated Wings Short Story)

Faded Realms

<u>**Thief of Hearts Co-write with Mila Young (complete series)**</u>

Darkest Destiny

Stolen Destiny

Broken Destiny

Sweet Destiny

<u>**Kingdom of Wolves Co-write with Mila Young**</u>

Wild Moon

Wild Heart

Wild Girl

Wild Love

Wild Soul

Wild Kiss

<u>**Stupid Boys Series Co-write with Rebecca Royce**</u>

Stupid Boys

Dumb Girl

Crazy Love

<u>**Breathe Me Duet Co-write with Ivy Fox (complete)**</u>

Breathe Me

Breathe You

Breathe Me Duet

<u>**Rich Demons of Darkwood Series Co-write with May Dawson**</u>

Make Me Lie

Make Me Beg

Make Me Wild

Make Me Burn

BOOKS BY MILA YOUNG

www.milayoungbooks.com

Savage

Lost Wolf

Broken Wolf

Fated Wolf

Cursed Wolf

Shadowlands

Shadowlands Sector, One

Shadowlands Sector, Two

Shadowlands Sector, Three

Shadows & Wolves Complete Collection

Monster and Me

Monster's Temptation

Monster's Obsession

The Devil's Gate MC

Rapture

Sin Demons

Playing With Hellfire

Hell In A Handbasket

All Shot To Hell

To Hell And Back

When Hell Freezes Over

Hell On Earth

Snowball's Chance In Hell

Kings of Eden

At the Mercy of Monsters

<u>Kings of Eden</u>

<u>Stolen Paradise</u>

Ruthless Lies

Chosen Vampire Slayer

Night Kissed

Moon Kissed

Blood Kissed

The Alpha-Hole Duet

Real Alphas Bite

Real Alphas Mate

Kingdom of Wolves

Wild Moon

Wild Heart

Wild Girl

Wild Love

Wild Soul

Wild Kiss

Wild Forever

Winter's Thorn

<u>To Seduce A Fae</u>

<u>To Tame A Fae</u>

<u>To Claim A Fae</u>

Shadow Hunters Series

Boxed Set 1

Gods and Monsters

Apollo Is Mine

Poseidon Is Mine

Ares Is Mine

Hades Is Mine

Haven Realm Series

Hunted (Little Red Riding Hood Retelling)

Cursed (Beauty and the Beast Retelling)

Entangled (Rapunzel Retelling)

Princess of Frost (Snow Queen)

<u>Thief of Hearts Series</u>

Dark Destiny

Stolen Destiny

Broken Destiny

Sweet Destiny

<u>Broken Souls Series</u>

School of Broken Souls

School of Broken Hearts

School of Broken Dreams

School of Broken Wings

Fallen World Series

Bound

Broken

Betrayed

Belong

Beautiful Beasts Academy

Manicures and Mayhem

Diamonds and Demons

Hexes and Hounds

Secrets and Shadows

Passions and Protectors

Ancients and Anarchy

Subscribe to Mila Young's Newsletter to receive exclusive content, latest updates, and giveaways. Join here.